Florence Hurd
Voyage of the Secret Duchess

WITHDRAWN

SILVER BAY PUBLIC LIBRARY
Silver Bay, Minn. 55614

 AVON
PUBLISHERS OF BARD, CAMELOT, DISCUS, EQUINOX AND FLARE BOOKS

THE VOYAGE OF THE SECRET DUCHESS is an original publication of Avon Books. This work has never before appeared in any form.

AVON BOOKS
A division of
The Hearst Corporation
959 Eighth Avenue
New York, New York 10019

Copyright © 1975 by Florence Hurd.
Published by arrangement with the author.

ISBN: 0-380-00353-8

All rights reserved, which includes the right
to reproduce this book or portions thereof in
any form whatsoever. For information address
Avon Books.

First Avon Printing, June, 1975.

AVON TRADEMARK REG. U.S. PAT. OFF. AND
FOREIGN COUNTRIES, REGISTERED TRADEMARK—
MARCA REGISTRADA, HECHO EN CHICAGO, U.S.A.

Printed in the U.S.A.

SILVER BAY PUBLIC LIBRARY
Silver Bay, Minn. 55614

First Hint of Terror

I began to prepare for bed. I was sitting at the dressing table brushing out my hair, trying to think of an amusing way I could present the evening's events to Adam, when suddenly I had the weird sensation I was being watched.

I remember pausing, the brush in my hand, while a cold chill ran up my arms. My eyes slid to Roxanne's doorway. There was nothing but shadow, a little rustle as she moved in her sleep.

A slight tapping sound behind me sent my heart flying to my mouth.

I turned. There, pressed against the ship's window, was a hand, a vivid yellow hand. No arm, no face, just a disembodied hand.

The next instant it was gone . . .

Avon Books by
Florence Hurd

THE SECRET OF AWEN CASTLE 18853 $ .95

CHAPTER ONE

Dusk has come and ahead of me there is a long, long night. Somehow, alone and afraid, I must pass through it. I have no one to talk to, no one to ask for advice—except Mathilda Jackson. Dear, kind Mathilda who has been my closest confidante on this long, terrifying voyage. But how can I go to her and reveal what is now tearing me apart? There are some things one does not speak of, even to the most cherished of friends.

So I sit here by lamplight in the dark of the moon listening to the creak of the ship, the wind in the sails, trying to sort through my whirling thoughts, thinking if I write the whole story down from the start, I might make sense of this terrible nightmare.

I cannot recall the precise moment I had my first feeling of impending disaster. It came and went so quickly, no more than a fleeting twist of the heart. Was it when I first looked upon *The Secret Duchess,* dismayed because it was a much older, much smaller and infinitely shabbier ship than I had expected? Or was it when I saw Sam Ching trundling his large, iron-hasped trunk up the gangway? It is hard to say, for whatever small forebodings I had were overshadowed in the excitement of our departure, the sounds of a ship getting underway at last—the whine of the winches, the shouts of the crew, the high whistle of the little tug standing by to lead us out of the Golden Gate.

This was not my first sea voyage—that had occurred some years earlier when I had crossed the Atlantic from my native England with my husband, Adam, and Roxanne, our daughter—but this was to be a new and very special adventure. Not only were we bound for China and Australia, places I had never been, but we were sailing on our very own vessel. *The Secret Duchess* was the fruition of Adam's boyhood dream, one he had not hoped to realize until he was well on in years. However, a few weeks short of his twenty-seventh birthday, he had unexpectedly fallen heir to a small legacy and by begging and borrowing had managed to scrape together supplemental funds to buy and refit, partially with steam, the sailing barque, *Duchess*. It was his first ship, his first command, and he was as proud of her as he would have been had she been the sleekest and swiftest of clippers.

Adam had been at sea since he was eighteen. His family, the Hayworths, descendants of a long line of gentry, were land poor and too impoverished to buy him a commission in the Navy, which, from their point of view, was the only proper maritime career for a gentleman. Adam had brine in his veins (as he has often told me) and so, over their protests, he joined the merchant fleet. By the time I met him he was twenty-two and first officer of the *Columbia*.

I can close my eyes now, look back on our first meeting and see him as he was then, standing at the punch bowl in the crystal-hung ballroom of our Hyde Park home—tall, burly shouldered, wearing an expression of intense boredom. It was my coming-out party, a cotillion, and we had crowds of people, many of whom I scarcely knew and have long since forgotten. He was somebody's cousin, a parrot-jawed girl with a silly laugh who had brought him along, I later discovered, as a possible partner should no one else ask her to dance. When she finally got round to introducing us, and the bored young man held my hand and smiled, I decided then and there he was going to be my husband.

It was not as easy as I thought. For one, I was the spoiled darling, the apple of a very rich father's eye. My younger brother, Randolph, only fifteen at the time, would be heir eventually to the Wiscombe Mills, but Papa wanted nothing less for his daughter—and he could well afford it—than a title. He, himself, had started out as the son of a humble draper and by sheer doggedness, boundless energy and keen business acumen had become a powerful figure in the business world. His marriage to Mama, the daughter of a famous solicitor, had gained him entry into high social circles and an earl or baronet as son-in-law would not only make me happy —so the reasoning went—but would permanently establish him as a man to be reckoned with.

The second obstacle to the fulfillment of my wish was a minor one: Adam. I had heard in a roundabout way that his intention was to remain a bachelor for life. He was a seaman, the sea was his career and there was no room in his life for a permanent alliance with a woman. That all changed, however, shortly after we met. To put it in terms used *ad nauseam* by the authors of those popular love stories I was addicted to at the time, he, poor darling, was struck by the same Cupid's arrow as myself.

The third hindrance to my becoming Mrs. Adam Hayworth, however, was far the most formidable. It was Mother Hayworth, a woman rigidly conscious of class, determined her son should not marry beneath him. But it was her very snobbishness which finally brought Papa round. The moment he learned that Mother Hayworth referred to me as that "draper's daughter," he gave us his blessing. Eventually Mother Hayworth capitulated also, but with the stipulation that there be a two-year engagement. The excuse given was my tender age—I was not yet nineteen—but I think she was hoping Adam would change his mind in the meanwhile—or better still that I would.

By this time, however, we were oblivious to the underhanded exchanges between Papa and Mother Hayworth (mostly by letter since Hayworth Hall was in Devon and the Hayworths rarely came to London). To Adam and me no one existed but ourselves. We were really, truly, daftly in love. The night before he was to sail on the *Columbia* we lost ourselves completely in that love. We were foolish, we were wicked, we were young. However we are—or were—to be judged we paid for our moments of happiness in bitter coin. Adam vowed we would be married as soon as he returned from his voyage. His ship was wrecked and he was mistakenly reported drowned at sea almost at the same moment I discovered I was with child. Papa found out and in true paternal outrage literally threw me out of the house.

What followed is a long, harrowing story involving an ancient secret society, the White Lady of Awen Castle, and the near death of my beloved Roxanne. It has all been told elsewhere and has no place in my present chronicle.* Suffice it to say Adam and I were eventually reunited and wed. Our opportune and happy marriage, however, did not wipe away my father's outrage, nor Mother Hayworth's haughtiness. So it was a welcome blessing when Adam's uncle offered him the position of first officer aboard one of his ships whose home port was San Francisco and we could leave all the unpleasantness behind.

In 1876 San Francisco was bustling, new, gaudy, still reeling with the excesses of the '49 gold rush and the later strikes in Montana and Dakota, the gilded stream always filtering

---

* *The White Lady of Awen Castle*

down to the city on the bay. It was a place of opera and theatre, of saloons and honky tonks, of jerry-built shacks and imposing mansions, of ragged derelicts and monied aristocrats wearing the newest fashions. I found the city exciting and would have loved it were it not for Adam's long absences at sea.

But now, we had the *Duchess* and we were together. Although Adam had cautioned me that as captain he would have grave responsibilities, that I might see little of him, that everything we owned in the world rode upon the success of this first endeavor, I could not help but picture our voyage as a second honeymoon, the man I loved by my side, the two of us sailing under azure skies across tranquil seas with a company of amiable passengers, and a happy, industrious crew.

Ah, how naive I was, how untried. How foolish.

Sam Ching was the last of the passengers to arrive. Roxanne and I were watching on the poop deck as he came up the gangway, pushing his baggage on a trolley. I saw Mr. Griggs, the second mate, speaking to him, gesticulating wildly and guessed that he was angry. Sam Ching was late and had delayed our departure by almost an hour. It strikes me odd now that all I ever saw of the little Chinese was the top of his straw coolie hat. I never had one glimpse of his face, never heard his voice, and except for that single uneasy twinge, never dreamed he was to become the core of my terror, the very essence of our disaster.

Watching him then, I only noted Mr. Griggs' anger, and as soon as Sam Ching disappeared from view into the alleyway, I dismissed him from my mind.

Roxanne, like any youngster of four, was beside herself with excitement, and I kept tight hold of her hand, fearing she would fall, or leap overboard, though her chin barely reached the rail.

"And where are we going, Mama?" she asked for the thousandth time.

"First we are going to Shanghai for tea, then to Australia for wool," I explained, also for the thousandth time.

"Lalia," she said, "Lalia," bouncing up and down. Roxanne was a great one for bouncing. She was exuberant, willful, somewhat pampered, I am afraid, but for all that a sweet and loving child. In looks she resembled me (in temperament, too, Adam said when she displeased him) with her auburn hair and gray-green eyes. I was hoping there would be another child close to Roxanne's age among the passengers. The voyage would be a long one and a playmate would relieve her tedium, but Adam had given me to understand that there would be none. Besides a cargo of lumber and furs we carried five passengers—a Mr. and Mrs. Thomas Hammersmith, missionaries, Bella Kincaid, opera singer, Mrs. Roderick Jackson, and, of course, Sam Ching.

"Look, Mama," said Roxanne, standing on tiptoe and pointing to a porpoise leaping out of the dark green water in a graceful arch, submerging, then a half minute later leaping out again a few yards ahead. It was almost as if the creature was guiding us out to sea.

"It is a porpoise or dolphin," I explained.

A man's voice behind us said, "A sign of good luck, so mariners like to think."

I turned. It was Jonathan Ralston, Adam's first mate, a tall, well built man, in his mid-thirties I judged. He might have been handsome, in a dark gypsy sort of way, if his expression were not so perpetually wooden. I had met him previously when Adam had brought him home for dinner one night. He had sat through the meal stony faced, saying little. I remember trying desperately to draw some conversation from him, but it was like pulling bent nails from ironwood. Obviously, from his speech he was English, an educated man, and when I asked him where he was born and where he had gone to school, he replied, "Plymouth," looking coldly, directly into my eyes. The look told me quite frankly he resented personal questions and I put him down as stand-offish and unsociable.

However, when at the end of the meal I left the two men to their cigars and port, I could hear him talking quite earnestly to Adam behind the closed door. And then I began to think it was my presence which had kept him aloof and speechless and that for some inexplicable reason he had taken an immediate dislike to me.

Later when I spoke to Adam about it, Adam pooh-poohed the idea. "Ralston is a seaman, been one all his life. He just does not feel comfortable in a dining room that is not rocking. Or at a table presided over by a lady."

"Oh?" I said, raising my eyebrows. "Perhaps he would have liked me better if I were some low woman . . ."

"Don't speak nonsense," Adam said.

"He has no wife, then?"

"I never asked, and I do not care a fig if he has one, three, or none. The man comes well recommended, is a fine seaman, a good navigator with a cool head and is totally trustworthy. Those are the things important to me." He settled back in his chair and picked up a newspaper. "You will get used to Mr. Ralston, I daresay, and find he is not such a bear, after all."

Perhaps Adam was right. For here was Mr. Ralston now, saying something pleasant, something about good luck.

"What a wonderful omen," I remarked.

"Good omens are what we shall need," he replied shortly, watching the dolphin with dark, somber eyes.

"You do not sound as if you anticipate a successful voyage, Mr. Ralston," I said teasingly.

He shrugged and was silent.

It was as if he had said his one good piece for the day and did not feel more was required of him. But I was not so easily put off. "Have you doubts about *The Secret Duchess?* Is she not seaworthy?"

"Oh, she's seaworthy enough." He turned his eyes upon me, cold and expressionless.

"What it is, then?" I could feel the chill wind of the open sea on my cheek. However Adam might defend Mr. Ralston, the man was a sour pessimist as well as a bear. "Is it the crew?"

"The crew is as able as one can get in these parts. They will do."

"But you anticipate some sort of trouble?"

He looked at me for a long time without speaking, and I began to grow a little irritated. "Surely if you think so, you are duty bound to speak up. My husband . . ."

"It is not a matter I feel I ought to discuss."

By now my exasperation, nudged along by anxiety, was impossible to hide. "Why do you not speak out, Mr. Ralston, and say what is on your mind?"

He looked at me again for a moment. "Very well, then. I do not like sailing on a ship with the captain's wife aboard."

"Oh," I said, thinking how right I had been about his resenting me. "Another sailor's superstition?"

"Partly, but one based on fact. Captains' wives should remain at home. A captain must have his mind on his ship twenty-four hours a day. It does no good to have distractions."

"I am a distraction, then?"

"You are his wife, you share his cabin."

I colored, catching the full meaning of his words. "I assure you, Mr. Ralston," I said, somewhat pompously, "I am fully aware of my husband's duties, his responsibilities. I have no intention of making myself a . . . a distraction, as you call it."

"It would be through no fault of yours. You are a very beautiful woman, Mrs. Hayworth," he said evenly, no sign of emotion in his voice nor in his eyes.

"Thank you for the compliment."

"It was not intended as one. Just a plain statement of fact."

Well, I had asked him to speak out. I wondered if the man was made entirely of stone, without feeling, without heart. "You are honest, that much I can say for you. But I could point out that my husband is not the only crew member with close family on board."

"You mean Mr. Griggs' son? But he is one of the hands. Billy is learning his father's trade and will be working hard enough. He'll not be underfoot."

"Meaning that I will be?"

"Madam, you take offense too easily," he said, looking away.

Roxanne who had remained silent during this interchange, looking from Mr. Ralston's face to my own, jerked at my hand. "Mama, Mama, let us see our cabin."

"Yes . . . yes, darling. If you will excuse us, Mr. Ralston?"

"By all means. You know your way, then? Captain Hayworth has asked me to escort you, if you did not . . ."

"Thank you, I do." I had been on the ship only once before when Adam had taken me on a quick tour, pointing out the passenger and officers' cabins. I knew it was below the poop, but there were two stairways, or ladders, as they were called aboard ship, and as I started to walk away, I could not remember for the life of me which one to take.

Mr. Ralston, noticing my hesitation, was at my side. "Let me show you," he said.

I accepted his offer with a cool nod. As we descended the stairs, I suddenly asked, "You dislike women, Mr. Ralston?"

"No. I like them very much—in their place."

And where is that, I wanted to ask, but remembering Mr. Ralston's penchant for honesty thought better of it. "There are other women aboard," I said.

"They are passengers."

"Part of the paying cargo, then?" I could not keep the sarcasm out of my voice.

"You must not take my remarks so personally, Mrs. Hayworth. You asked my opinion, I gave it. Quite truthfully I would prefer no passengers at all on a small ship."

"I have not met them yet, but they sound like a harmless lot. Missionaries, an opera singer. Or perhaps you object to the Chinese gentleman?"

We had reached the cabin door. Mr. Ralston opened it and Roxanne scooted in ahead.

"I do not share the common prejudices against Orientals," he said. "But he has already had a slight dispute with Mr. Griggs."

"He was late."

"Yes. But the dispute was over his trunk."

"His trunk? Why should Mr. Griggs be upset because of that?"

"I thought you knew."

"No, no. Is there some contraband he's trying to smuggle out of the country?"

"I can see no harm in telling you, since I am sure the whole ship knows by now. It is not contraband. The trunk contains a dead man."

Then Mr. Ralston turned and walked away.

CHAPTER TWO

My first impulse was to laugh. Mr. Ralston was joking. A dead man, indeed! The dour first mate's parting statement had been his idea of humor, a grim witticism aimed at shivering my supposedly frail, feminine bones.

After a few moments' reflection, however, I realized Jonathan Ralston, with his solemn, sober air, his habit of speaking to the point, was not a man to jest. If he said there was a corpse in Ching's trunk, then there must be one. And again I felt that little twist of anxiety, a doubt, an uneasy pinch at my nerves. Surely Adam would have some explanation?

In the meanwhile Roxanne was clamoring for my attention. She had found the bunk especially conducive to her favorite form of exercise and was jumping up and down on it pretending she was skipping rope. "Look, Mama!" she shouted. "Look at me!"

I lifted her off. "None of that," I scolded sharply. "You will have to mind your manners and behave like a young lady. You must remember you are the captain's daughter."

"Yes, Mama." Her eyes went immediately round and solemn. I wondered if I was being overly harsh with her. She was hardly more than a baby, and yet a little sternness would not harm her. It was going to be difficult enough, in view of Ralston's resentment, without having Roxanne performing like a circus clown.

Great tears began to form in those large green eyes. "Well then," I said briskly, resisting the urge to take her in my arms, "let us see what our home is to be like for the next few weeks."

The original captain's cabin had been enlarged, so that it now occupied the space of two—still far from a spacious room—but pleasant enough. It was fitted out with a double bunk, a fixed dressing table which could also be used as a desk, two comfortable overstuffed chairs, and several built-in cupboards. There was a round porthole giving a view of the sea, and on the door another one with muslin curtains drawn back. Our cabin led directly into a tiny cubby hole of a room, once a pantry, and now converted for Roxanne's use. The outer door had been boarded up, but there was a porthole on the sea side to give light. Roxanne, her admonishment forgotten, was very pleased to have a cabin for her very own, complete with tiny dressing table, bunk and a set of drawers beneath it.

Adam had not only rebuilt our cabin, but he had put in several passenger cabins in addition to those of the two officers who shared our quarters. As a consequence the dining saloon, ordinarily centrally located with each door opening on to it, had been eliminated, and had been replaced by a passage, or alleyway. The dining saloon itself, was now beneath the main deck, 'tween decks in marine parlance, reached by a short flight of stairs.

I am describing all this because the layout is crucial as to what happened later.

Despite the expansion of living room, I could see we would all be living cheek by jowl, and although Adam had thoughtfully thickened the walls between each cabin so that we need not speak in constant whispers, I realized any loud sounds could be heard from one end of the quarters to the other. Another reason I must try to restrain Roxanne's effusiveness.

Shortly after eleven the steward came to the door. He was a man in his fifties, stooped at the shoulders, with a fluff of white sideburns at each side of a long, yellow face. His sallow skin gave him the appearance of a man who suffered from recurring bouts of fever, which, indeed, turned out to be the case.

"I beg your pardon," he said politely. "I am afraid we shall not be serving in the saloon until this evening. The cook is having some difficulty with the stove. I can bring you some cold meat and bread in the meantime."

"Thank you," I said. "That will be fine."

I did not see Adam until three that afternoon. He looked tired, newly sunburned, but happy. "Well, what do you think of her?" he asked gleefully, like a small boy with his first Sunday suit.

"She is beautiful," I said, all my small misgivings evaporating in the light of his radiant smile. He kissed me.

"You didn't mind my not being here to take you aboard?" he asked.

"Not in the least," I said.

"The business of getting underway is sometimes complicated. But we are out to sea now with a good stiff wind."

He drew off his jacket and hung it neatly from a hook, extracting a cigar from the inner pocket. "Have you met the others?" he asked.

"No. But I hope to at dinner."

"I think I can promise you fairly good meals. Much better than on most ships of this sort. Cookie has sailed with me before."

"Cookie?"

"All ship's cooks are known as Cookie, just as the carpenters are all called Chips. I don't know what Cookie's real name is—he is Chinese—but he does make a fine stew."

"The steward said there was some difficulty with the galley stove . . ."

"Yes, and you can be sure I've heard about it from Cookie himself. But it's all fixed now. And he's quite happy among his pots and pans."

He lit a cigar and in the match's flare I saw thin lines of strain at the corners of his eyes. "Did Mr. Ralston show you to the cabin?" he asked.

"Yes. He said something funny."

"Funny? Mr. Ralston?"

"He said that the Chinese passenger, Sam Ching, had . . . had . . . a dead man in the trunk he carried aboard."

Adam looked at me for a moment, startled, and then he began to laugh. He laughed as I have never seen him laugh before, sputtering and coughing over his cigar. I joined in, as did Roxanne, although neither of us were quite sure what the merriment was all about. When Adam had spent himself he said, "It is true enough. It is very true. There is a dead man in that trunk. Ching's father, Ah. The old man died, and like a dutiful Chinese son, Sam is taking his father's ashes back to Canton for burial."

"I do not think it is such a joke," I said, somewhat disconcerted. "Why did not Mr. Ralston tell me so in the first place?"

"He is a man of few words, I suppose." Sober now, Adam gazed intently at the tip of his cigar. "You are right. It is not all that funny. I would have much preferred had the matter been hushed. But Mr. Griggs was angry at Ching for being late. He made some uncouth remark about 'chucking his filthy trunk overboard,' and Sam retaliated by saying he was not to touch it as it contained his father's honorable ashes. Of course, that sent Griggs off again."

"But why? I should think Ching has a perfect right to protect his trunk."

"The way of it, my dear Charlotte, is that sailors are a very superstitious lot. They do not like having a dead man aboard, even if he has been reduced to a handful of ashes."

"And you are not superstitious?"

"No. You ought to know that by now. I don't believe in ghosts, curses, or palm reading. Superstition is hogwash." He stamped out his cigar and lay back on the bunk, closing his eyes.

Roxanne who had been standing by his side, tugged at his hand. "Papa, Papa!"

"What is it, darling?" he asked, opening one eye.

"I saw a . . . I saw a . . ." She looked to me questioningly.

"A dolphin," I supplied.

"I saw a dolphin."

"Did you now? How grand. You know that is a sign of good luck, don't you?" He closed the eye again.

She nodded vigorously.

I smiled. "So you are not superstitious," I teased. "It is all hogwash."

He did not answer and, looking down at him, I saw he was sound asleep.

That night I met the passengers.

Roxanne had an early supper and I put her to bed at seven-thirty. Adam, after an hour's sleep, had gone back to the bridge, so that when I went down to the dining saloon for dinner I went alone. Adam had informed me there was to be no quibbling, no snobbishness, no hard feelings as to who would have the privilege of being seated at the captain's table. Officers and passengers were to eat together. (The crew, of course, ate in the forecastle.) The reason for this was quite simple: The saloon was too small to accommodate more than one large, round table and eight chairs. The only other furnishing was a long bench upholstered in faded red velvet under the windows.

When I arrived two of the women were already there. They introduced themselves: Mrs. Kincaid and Mrs. Jackson. Two such disparate females I have never sat down to dinner with. Both were past youth, long past, I saw at a glance, but Mrs. Kincaid had made a valiant, if not entirely successful, attempt to hide the passage of years with a liberal application of powder and rouge. She was all baubles and jangles and rings, and her stout figure was stuffed tightly into a gown of shimmering satin, one that would have been far more suitable for a Court gala than a meal in our poor, shabby saloon.

"Call me Bella," she said at once, squeezing my hand with her beringed one.

Mrs. Jackson, on the other hand, wore no jewelry except for a plain gold wedding band and a brooch at her throat. Her drab, faded, dark blue dress fit her spare figure neatly and without fuss. Her face was lined and browned by the sun, her hands rough and knobbed, the hands of a woman who has worked hard with them all her life.

"If we are going to be on a first name basis," Mrs. Jackson said, smiling at me with candid blue eyes, "I am Mathilda."

I told them mine.

The contrast between the two women was not only in appearance, but in manner as well. Whereas Bella Kincaid moved, twitched and twittered, constantly shifting on her chair (perhaps because of her corsets), there was a quiet repose about Mathilda, a lovely serenity which I envied. It drew me to her instantly.

Bella Kincaid leaned forward. "Aren't we going to meet our handsome captain tonight?"

"I'm afraid not," I smiled. "He is particularly anxious to see things go right on our first night out."

"Good," said Bella. "I like a man in charge who takes his work seriously."

"You are an experienced voyager?" I asked her.

"I'd say I was. Made the trip around the Cape from New York in 'fifty-five, and a rough one it was."

Mathilda spoke up. "This is my first."

"You are not nervous about it?" I asked.

"Of course not, my dear," Mathilda Jackson assured me. "I've not been to sea, but we—my husband, Roddy, and me—have seen plenty of danger living and working as we did in the mining camps."

"Really?" said Bella. "I've done a trick or two in the Sierra."

The door opened behind us and turning I saw a man and woman standing on the threshold. He was very tall, thin, with a face resembling a sorrowful hound, grooved and dewlapped. The woman—if you could call her that, for she looked no older than a child of twelve—clung to his arm, her eyes, under a mop of curls, extraordinarily large holding an expression of fearful expectancy.

"Mr. and Mrs. Hammersmith?" Mathilda inquired.

"That is us," said the man in a deep mellifluous voice. "I am sorry we are late. But my wife was feeling a bit queasy and did not know if she wanted dinner."

"I'm quite all right now," Mrs. Hammersmith said in a tiny voice, looking up at her husband. Her prominent teeth fitted badly in her small face, and were it not for her beautiful eyes, a deep, almost purple blue, she would have been quite homely.

I was watching her, those eyes in particular, when I saw them suddenly widen in shock, then narrow, as her face flushed a deep red. It all happened so fast, the surprise, the wary, almost cunning contraction of the eyes, I would not have believed I saw any of it except for the tell-tale red still lingering in her cheeks.

I wondered what had caused that odd reaction when I noticed Bella Kincaid staring boldly at Mrs. Hammersmith. Perhaps the two women had met previously and their meeting or association had not been a pleasant one. But if that were so neither made any open acknowledgment of ever having known one another when the introductions went round. It occurred to me then that Mrs. Hammersmith's shock, or revulsion, was due to her outraged, religious sensibilities at Mrs. Kincaid's flamboyant appearance. Apparently her husband shared his wife's view for he snubbed Bella Kincaid, addressing all his remarks either to me or Mrs. Jackson.

"And what is your destination?" he asked Mathilda.

"Shanghai," she answered. "And I am as excited as punch at the prospect. My husband, Roddy, has obtained a fine position there as an agent for Kimberly's, you know."

Mr. Hammersmith did not know.

"Export-import. Tea and china and laquered what-nots. He has sent for me." She sighed. "I still can't believe our good fortune. We've worked so hard all these years, always side by side, and nothing we turned our hands to seemed to come right. Then Roddy went to work for Mr. Kimberly, and in less than a year he had learned the business so well Mr. Kimberly sent him to Shanghai as one of his agents."

During this explanation by Mathilda, Mr. Ralston had come into the saloon and, giving a brief nod, seated himself at the table.

Bella, who had been eyeing him, said, "And who are you?"

"First mate," he said. "Mr. Ralston."

There was a murmur of names all round, then a brief silence as the steward entered and began to serve the first course.

Mr. Hammersmith cleared his throat. "Your good fortune, Mrs. Jackson, is testimony to one of my strongest beliefs. God rewards those whose hard work and diligence merits it."

"I do believe so," said Mathilda sincerely, her seamed face beaming. "I earnestly believe so. And where are you bound?"

"Canton," he said. "We are going to do God's work among the heathen there. We—my wife and I—are fortunate too, in that we were chosen among many others to answer the call."

Bella, who was not one to be ignored for too long, spoke up. "So you are going to convert the heathen Chinee, are you? Well. And did you know we have one on board with us? You could start with him. What is his name, Charlotte?"

"Sam Ching," I said.

"Yes, I am aware of Sam Ching," said Mr. Hammersmith. "But I do not think he is the only one aboard ship who is in need of the Lord's guidance." He gave Bella a meaningful glance.

The barb was not lost on her. "How true," she said sweetly. "Did you have anyone special in mind?" She glanced at Mrs. Hammersmith who had not spoken a word throughout but sat staring down into her untouched plate.

There was an uncomfortable silence.

I ought to say something, I thought, make some attempt to turn the talk on to a safer, more neutral subject. But as often happens at such moments my mind was a perverse blank.

Mrs. Jackson, however, bless her heart, came to the rescue. "I see a place has been set for Mr. Ching. Maybe he'll tell us he's already become a Christian."

Bella pressed her lips together. "I doubt he'll join us."

"How is that?" I inquired.

"Why, he knows better than to eat with white folk."

Mr. Hammersmith took up his napkin and wiped his mouth slowly, deliberately, all the while fixing Bella with a stern eye. "And you think yourself superior to this poor man?"

"Superior or not," said Bella, "he's not a poor man. None of them are, though they pretend to be. I'll wager that trunk of his is filled to the brim with gold."

"No," I began to protest.

They all looked at me and I turned scarlet. "If . . ." I went on. ". . . if there was anything of value . . . he would have asked the captain to put it in the ship's safe."

"My dear Charlotte," said Bella. "You don't think he would *declare* it, do you?"

Mr. Ralston, who as yet had not spoken, made a sound in the back of his throat. "It seems to me," he said, "everyone is assuming a great deal. If the man has gold, I, for one, could hardly blame him for not declaring it. The Chinese have been much maligned in California. I wonder if any of you were aware that they were the first in the gold fields? No, of course not. How could you? They were always driven off by the superior 'white folk.' No matter how far back into the hills the Chinese went they were trailed by a half dozen prospectors counting on Chinese luck to lead them to pay dirt. The Chinese, even now, are constantly harried by laws and regulations hurriedly passed to force them out, not to speak of outright murder and banditry to which they are subject. And the terrible part is these robbers are never punished. Did you know a Chinese cannot testify in court?" He looked around the table.

I was astonished at Mr. Ralston's outburst, not at what he said, as much that he made such an emotional speech at all.

"And now," he said, getting to his feet, "if you will excuse me, I have matters to attend to."

Mr. Hammersmith carefully placed his knife and fork side by side on his empty plate. "Speaking of gold and trunks," he said, "the bosun, a Mr. Phipps, told me earlier today that the trunk contained Mr. Ching's father's ashes. It seems the Chinese have an obsession about being buried on their native soil, which I can understand. But the soul, that poor soul has never come to accept God's word . . ."

"God's word," said Bella, reaching for her wine glass. "The beginning and end of all."

Mr. Hammersmith turned a deep red. "It would seem to me you are the last person in the world to mock."

"Is that so?" Bella bristled. "Well, Mr. Hammersmith, let me tell you . . ."

She was interrupted by the clink and clatter of a glass falling to the floor. Mrs. Hammersmith was on her feet, swaying, her face ghastly pale. "I . . . I don't feel well, Thomas . . ."

Mr. Hammersmith immediately rose and took her arm. "I am so sorry, my dear. Of course, I should have realized . . ." He put his arm about her and helped her through the door.

"He's got his nerve," Bella grumbled after they had gone.

"I'm sure Mr. Hammersmith did not mean to aim his remarks at you," I said, trying to smooth things over.

"He most certainly did," said Bella irritably.

"Now, now," said Mathilda soothingly. "The man's a preacher. It's his natural way of speaking."

"That's all very well for you to say," said Bella. "*You* worked hard—as if I didn't—and you got a halo round your head."

Mathilda, calmly munching on a biscuit, said nothing.

The dinner I had eaten began to churn in my stomach. "Mrs. Kincaid," I began, swallowing hard. "Bella . . . I can see where you are a sensitive person, and maybe Mr. Hammersmith was somewhat tactless. But we are going to be together for many weeks and would not it be better if we all tried to get along?"

"Charlotte is right," Mathilda said. "If the man rubs you the wrong way, ignore him. Now here we are on a fine ship, good food, good wine, and Charlotte and me for good company. So why not make the best of it."

"If you put it that way . . ." She shrugged her shoulders and emptied her wine glass.

"Are you going to Shanghai too?" Mathilda asked.

"No, Melbourne. I plan to open a boardinghouse. I am tired of opera. Besides, there's not much money in it. I'm told there's a shortage of good boardinghouses in Australia, and I think I'll try my hand at it."

"It can be profitable," said Mrs. Jackson noncommittally.

"I hope so," Bella pushed herself away from the table. "Now if you ladies will pardon me. I think I'll go to my cabin. This particular corset I'm wearing never did fit me right."

When she had gone Mathilda reached across the table and squeezed my hand. "You're still frowning. Don't fret so."

"I don't want any unpleasantness among the passengers."

"It's not your fault we drew such a mixed bag."

"Perhaps I ought to have a talk with Mr. Hammersmith."

She shook her head sadly. "My dear, you must be a very sheltered creature not to have sized up the situation at once, even if you did not know about Mrs. Kincaid."

"Know? Know what?"

"First off, the name Bella Kincaid is only one of the names she goes by."

"You mean it is her professional name? The name she uses on the opera stage?"

Mathilda laughed. "That woman was never in opera. I doubt she could sing a note if she tried."

My heart began to flutter. "She is a thief . . . a criminal?"

"There's a good many who wouldn't consider her profession a crime, but a benefit to society. That is male society."

A light suddenly dawned. Of course—the flamboyant clothes, the jangling bracelets, the earloops, the paste necklace. "She's a . . ."

"A parlor house madam. Known sometimes as Mother Belle, Belle Thorpe, Beatrice King. I read all about her in the papers. Her last place was on Stockton Street, very notorious."

I was not all that naive. I had been aware those places existed. Everyone who lived any length of time in San Francisco knew. I remembered a thundering sermon given by the Reverend Fuller one Sunday. "Prostitution," he had declaimed from the pulpit, "is a scourge. And it receives as much encouragement and support from men of families as from the unmarried." I could understand why Mr. Hammersmith seemed disturbed.

"I've had a rough and tumble life," Mathilda was saying. "I've met all kinds. And I can spot one of *them* a mile off. But her, I know about in particular, because her picture was in the papers. It was quite a scandal. She and all her girls were arrested, and she was given the choice of a fine and jail sentence or leaving town. Some say she was made an example. But Roddy didn't believe so. He thinks it was the conniving between the chief of police and another madam who wanted her business. You see Ma Belle had an elegant house, the most beautiful girls in the city and a very rich clientele."

"I had no idea . . ."

"Shocks you?"

"A little," I smiled.

"Don't let it. My motto is live and let live. There's room for all of us."

And on that note we parted company for the night.

Roxanne was sleeping soundly when I looked in on her. She lay on her back, one small, white arm crooked over her tousled head, the blankets all in a heap at her feet. I pulled them up gently, covering her, and she stirred, a smile quivering on her lips. She looked so fragile, so innocent, and I thought of the dinner conversation, the swirl of barbed talk and sly innuendo, and wondered if it would be wise to expose her to that sort of atmosphere. It was not Bella's profession which worried me as much as Hammersmith's harping at the woman. But then Roxanne had been promised she might have breakfast and luncheon in the dining saloon, and to revoke that promise would certainly cause more "Why, Mamas?" than Hammersmith speaking of converting sinners and heathens to the ways of the Lord.

Once that was settled in my mind I began to prepare for bed. I was sitting at the dressing table brushing out my hair, trying to think of an amusing way I could present the evening's events to Adam, when suddenly I had the weird sensation I was being watched. I remember pausing, the brush in my hand, while a cold chill ran up my arms. My eyes slid to Roxanne's doorway. There was nothing but shadow, a little rustle as she moved in her sleep.

A slight tapping sound behind me sent my heart flying into my mouth. I turned. There pressed against the window was a hand, a vivid yellow hand. No arm, no face, just a disembodied hand.

The next instant it was gone.

CHAPTER THREE

I sat there for a long time staring at the window, empty now except for the glimmer of reflected light in the alleyway. After a while I began to wonder if I had seen anything at all. My heart still fluttering, I plucked up enough courage to go to the door and, opening it, cautiously peered out. The passage was empty.

Overwrought, overtired, that was it. The hand had been sheer fancy culled up by a weary brain. I was glad I had not screamed or called out, raising an alarm. A hysterical female, Mr. Ralston would have dubbed me. I fastened the door and drew the curtains.

It was not until the next morning I had the chance to speak to Adam. He had come in at midnight the evening before literally drooping with fatigue and had fallen asleep the moment his head touched the pillow. Now, much refreshed over a cup of morning tea, he asked me how my meeting with the passengers had gone. I went into my amusing little story then, explaining Bella Kincaid's real profession and the Hammersmiths' reaction to it.

Adam, however, did not seem to see any comedy in the situation. He neither laughed nor smiled. "I suspected something like that when Thomas Hammersmith came up to the poop deck last night. He informed me he and his wife would not eat in the dining saloon. 'We want our meals in our cabin,' he said, as if he were giving orders to the headwaiter at the Palace. I wanted to tell him *The Secret Duchess* was not a grand ocean steamer on which one pays a good deal more for personal service. What I did say was, 'We have only one steward, Mr. Hammersmith, to serve us all. He is not a young man, as you may have noticed, and I cannot burden him with extra duties.'

" 'But Sam Ching was brought his dinner,' he came back at me.

" 'That is because our cook is also Chinese and he does

not mind waiting on his countryman.'" Adam set his cup down and filled it again from the pot.

I said, "I wondered why we did not see Mr. Ching at the table last night."

"Cookie says he prefers to keep to his cabin altogether."

Remembering our conversation at the dinner table, I could understand why the little Chinese might feel that way. "But the Hammersmiths. . . ." I began.

"They will just have to make do," Adam said in a tone of exasperation. "Charlotte, it is up to you to play hostess and try to keep the Hammersmiths and that Kincaid woman from each other's throats."

"I tried . . . but if you were only there . . ."

"I cannot be there all of the time, not even most of the time," he said irritably. "I have never known so many things to go wrong the first day out. A stuck jib, two broken braces, a stubborn galley stove. Complaints from the cook all the way up. I tell you I have too much on my mind to be bothered by some missionaries and a parlor house madam." And with that he got up and strode from the cabin.

I could only stare at the closed door, openmouthed. Adam, for the most part, was a rather easy going, reasonable person, and to see him flare up was a rare thing. I made a firm resolve, then and there, to speak only of pleasantries and to keep silent on whatever problems arose, whether with the passengers or myself. I had so looked forward to this voyage, our time together after years of Adam's long absences, I was not going to let anything, or anyone come between us.

Of course, what I did not know then was that *The Secret Duchess* had already done that.

Roxanne was impatient for breakfast, her first visit to the saloon, and so we left the cabin before the summons of the bell which announced our meals. "We shall be the first ones," I told her. But when we entered the saloon Mathilda Jackson was seated at the table knitting, pulling the wool from a large string bag at her feet.

"I see you are an early riser," I said.

"Always was," she smiled. "Up before dawn for so many years, I can't shake the habit." She leaned over and patted Roxanne's head. "So this is your kitten. What a pretty girl."

Roxanne leaned against me, blushing. "Say 'thank you,' darling, for the nice compliment."

"Thank you for the nice compliment," Roxanne dutifully repeated.

"It's a lovely day," said Mrs. Jackson. "The sunrise over the sea was something to watch."

"I hope the others share your good mood," I said.

"It's my guess," she said, putting her needles back into the bag, "we won't see Madam Kincaid this early. She's got her routine, too, turned round from mine, but a routine. When I was doing laundry up in Pine Hill, one of our customers was a . . ." She gave a sidelong glance at Roxanne. ". . . a boardinghouse lady and she had a fit if she was disturbed before one in the afternoon."

The breakfast bell rang, and a few minutes later the Hammersmiths arrived, followed by Mr. Ralston and Mr. Griggs, the second mate. Up close Mr. Griggs proved to be a man of medium height with grizzled whiskers and a nervous blink to his bulging brown eyes. When I introduced the passengers, he growled something and sat down.

Immediately the steward entered and began to serve. For a few minutes we were all absorbed in our meal. I helped Roxanne by cutting up her bread and pouring cream on her porridge, nodding encouragement when, after a few fumbling tries, she managed to hold the spoon right. The silence continued, interrupted only by the clink of cutlery and Mr. Griggs' noisy chewing as he bolted his food.

I turned to Mrs. Hammersmith. "You are feeling better?" I inquired politely.

"Much," she said.

Silence descended again. Even Roxanne seemed to have become mute.

"Thick-skinned clodhoppers," Mr. Griggs suddenly mumbled into his coffee cup.

"What? What's that?" Mrs. Jackson inquired.

Mr. Griggs looked up at her across the table, a little surprised. "Nothin'. Just speakin' to myself."

"Who are you referring to?" said Mr. Hammersmith in an offended voice.

"Beggin' your pardon, Reverend. Nothin' to do with you. Was referrin' to the crew."

"Am I given to understand our ship is being manned by clodhoppers, as you call them?" Mr. Hammersmith wanted to know.

Mr. Ralston answered him. "Not entirely. There are a few rotten apples. All crews have them."

"Worthless scrapin's of the waterfront," Mr. Griggs muttered, blinking rapidly. "Don't hold a candle to my Billy. Billy's my son. He's not A.B. yet, but he's strong and he's willin' to learn. Those others, all thumbs, as useless as livin' ballast."

"They will be kicked into shape soon enough," said Mr. Ralston. "There is nothing like a long voyage to turn a clodhopper into a good hand."

At the mention of hand, I started. Suddenly, and without quite knowing why, I recalled the hand I had seen at my window, or thought I had seen. And I found myself staring at Mr. Ralston's. Neither of his hands were the least like the one which had frightened me so, nor were Mr. Griggs' or Mr. Hammersmith's. It had been short and thick fingered and yellow, not a human hand at all. Of course, I realized belatedly, it was *not* a human hand; it was a glove. Anyone could have worn it, even a woman. My eyes shifted to Bella's ringed fingers, and then to Mathilda Jackson's work-worn hands before I caught myself. It was a fantasy, remember? Why should anyone don a yellow glove and tap at my window to frighten me? The thought was absurd.

"And then there's the Chinaman," Mr. Griggs complained. "With a dead man in that blasted trunk of his."

"Does it disturb you so much?" I asked Mr. Griggs.

"I heard the dead man . . . Ah Ching was his name . . ." He paused dramatically, blinking all around. ". . . was murdered."

We were all duly shocked, except for Mr. Ralston who did not turn a hair. "You seem to know more about it than I do," he said. "And how did your informant come to that conclusion?"

"Cookie told him." Mr. Griggs brought his coffee cup to his lips with a trembling hand. "I don't like it. I don't like it. I told the cap'n I didn't like it."

"It doesn't bother me," said Mathilda Jackson in her usual placid tone. "You read about them Chinese tong wars in the papers all the time. One of them is always getting a knife stuck in his back."

"It's bad, very bad," Mr. Griggs mumbled. "A man that's murdered never stays easy in his grave."

"He isn't in his grave yet," Mrs. Jackson pointed out cheerfully.

Mr. Griggs' blinking eyes gazed at her mournfully. "Them that's been murdered is unsettled. They walk. They . . ."

"Mr. Griggs!" Mr. Ralston interrupted, his mouth a thin, hard line. "Let that kind of talk stay in the forecastle."

Mr. Griggs stared at him for a moment, his lips moving

soundlessly. Then spluttering something about "young 'uns still wet behind the ears," he rose and left the table.

"I suppose," said Mr. Hammersmith, "he resents serving under a man much younger than he."

Since both Adam and Ralston were obviously Mr. Griggs' junior he could have been referring to either.

"Mr. Griggs has his quirks," said Ralston. "But he's a pretty fair seaman."

I had to credit Mr. Ralston for defending his second mate, despite his earlier reprimand. But I could not help wondering if Ralston, too, took exception to Adam's youth. Here was a man obviously intelligent, a good navigator, according to Adam, one who had been at sea all his life. Why was it he did not have his own command by now, instead of serving under a young captain on a small, not very up-to-date ship?

I was musing over this during a general silence when Mr. Ralston, with a curt nod, got up and left the saloon.

"Mr. Griggs seems to think we'll have a ghost," said Mathilda, her eyes twinkling. "At least the voyage won't be without a little excitement."

"If the dead man walks," said Mr. Hammersmith pontifically. "It is because he died unbaptized and nothing else."

"Surely you don't believe in ghosts, Mr. Hammersmith?" I asked.

"I certainly do," he said emphatically.

"Have you ever seen one?" I inquired, and even as I did so I wondered why a cold wind seemed to pass across my heart. It was all idle talk.

"No," he answered. "Nor have I ever seen the Lord. But that does not mean that neither exist."

"I've seen one," Mathilda chimed in, good humoredly.

"You are not serious," I said lightly, knowing full well she was.

"Cross my heart. I saw him, the ghost, plainly as I'm seeing you. It was in a place called California Gulch. Roddy and me rented the floor above a saloon with the idea of running a hotel, and we was thrilled to get it because the rent was so cheap. Soon we began to wonder why no one stayed but for a day or two. And then one night I was roused out of sleep by a hollering in the front room. Now the front room was empty, that is, we had no lodgers there at the time. I got up without waking Roddy, thinking some drunk had wandered upstairs and was getting himself a free bed.

"When I opened the door I got the shock of my life. There wasn't much light, only the lamp from the hall, but I saw a man, his left cheek laid bare with a cut so wide, I swear you could have put a fist in it. And the blood was streaming down his clothes and dripping on the floor. He opened his mouth like he was yelling for help, but no sound came. I said, 'You've been hurt bad. Let me get some light so I can see.' I ran out and unhooked the lamp from the wall, and when I got back he was gone.

"I looked carefully around. The bed was made up, like I had done it two days before. There was no sign that anybody had been in that room, let alone a man bleeding to death. Not one drop of blood on the carpet or anywhere, though I crawled twice around the floor on my hands and knees. I did a lot of asking after that. And the saloon keeper finally admitted I had seen the ghost of a man named Baker. He had been robbed of his gold and murdered in that room a year before."

"Very interesting," said Mr. Hammersmith. "I have heard many stories like that."

"It's true. Every word is gospel."

Mr. Hammersmith gave her a stern look and she colored. "I am sure it is," he said. "One expects that sort of thing from those who have died without God's word, God's solace. I, myself, have done the rounds of those boom towns, the camps. Pits of licentiousness, debauchery, pollution, loathsome diseases, profanity, drunkenness . . ." Mr. Hammersmith's eyes took on a peculiar fire as his voice rose to a ringing tone. ". . . prostitution. But one does not turn one's back on the Lord's vineyard, no matter how bitter and unpromising the grapes. Yes, with all modesty, I can say I was able to sweeten and harvest not a few of those shriveled souls for the glory of everlasting life."

There was a momentary silence and then Mathilda brought her hands together in a little ripple of applause. "Well put."

Mr. Hammersmith nodded his head and smiled graciously.

I had meant to say nothing to Adam about our talk of ghosts and murder. It was Roxanne who did. She and Adam were sitting together on the bunk, Adam, with a piece of string stretched between his thumbs, teaching her the tricks of a cat's cradle, when Roxanne suddenly asked, "What is a ghost, Papa?"

Adam looked up at me in surprise. Truthfully, I was as surprised as he, for I had thought Roxanne, playing with her rag dolly on the bench under the window, was too busily engrossed to have heard a word spoken at the table. "Little pitchers have big ears," I remarked.

"Mrs. Jackson said she saw a ghost," Roxanne explained.

"She has a fine imagination," Adam said. "Ghosts, my dear little one, are fancies."

"Like fairy princesses?"

"Like fairy princesses. Now you take the string into your room and see what you can do with it. I would like to talk to your mother for a bit."

Adam shut the door of the little cubby hole. "Now," he said in a low voice, "what is this about ghosts?"

I gave him a brief account of our morning's conversation and how Mr. Griggs' gloomy remarks had started it.

"I might have known," he said, sitting down on a chair. "Perhaps it was unwise of me to take Sam Ching on. But, poor chap, no one else would and Cookie—he is a relative of some sort—begged me too."

"Good-hearted Adam," I said, kissing the top of his head.

"Well, it's too late now. If they did not have Sam Ching to grumble and gossip over, there would be something or someone else."

"Did you know beforehand Ching's father was murdered?" I said in a voice barely above a whisper.

"No. Mr. Griggs asked me the same. He was very upset about it. A very nervous man, that Griggs."

"The cook seems to have told one of the crew who told . . ."

"Cookie ought to keep his mouth shut." He tore the wrappings from a fresh cigar.

"Do you think he really knows?"

"He may. The point is it's an ugly rumor to be spreading on a ship. It's bad for discipline."

"Do you expect trouble, Adam?"

"Not while I am at the helm," he said grimly.

If trouble was brewing one would have never known. The weather sparkled with sun and sea as we sailed calmly, slowly, gracefully under pellucid skies. The talk at luncheon and dinner was again of phantoms, Mathilda Jackson and Mr. Hammersmith vying with one another in their tales taken from the legendary lore of the mountains. Most of the stories were quite humorous and we laughed a good deal, but underneath the laughter, at least mine, there was a note of uneasiness.

That uneasiness seemed to grow stronger when I was alone in our cabin that night. It was late—well past midnight—and

I could not sleep. Roxanne was in her bunk, and Adam was in the chart-room. Every now and then I would go to the door and peek out. The chart-room was directly across the alleyway, and I could see the light under the sill. Soon I began to wonder if Adam had not fallen asleep over his maps, and it was difficult to resist the temptation to knock at the door. But I must not interfere. I must not, as Ralston had put it, be a "distraction."

My uneasiness, my anxiety, increased, although I really could not think why. The ship was very quiet. The only sounds were a steady creaking of wood and the far away thump of the engines. The engines had been turned on sometime during dinner because, as Mr. Ralston explained, we had run into a calm. Mathilda thought it wonderful that we should have the advantage of both steam and sail, since our passage and her reunion with Roddy would be that much quicker.

I had opened the door for perhaps the tenth time when a sound made me turn my head. In the dim light it seemed there was a figure at Sam Ching's cabin window—the end one in the passage—but when I poked my head out all the way, I saw that my "figure" was only a shadow cast by a swinging lamp. I went and sat on the bed again. After a bit my nerves got the better of me. In my jumpy state of mind the cabin appeared to grow smaller and smaller until I felt the very walls would squeeze the breath out of me. I pulled on a dressing gown and let myself out the door.

The night was soft and mysterious. High up a pale, misted moon rode the naked spars, casting the ship's opaque shadow on the glassy shimmer of sea. A riding light burned clear and untroubled on the far end of the ship, like a tiny, bright star. I saw no one and presently, for some reason, the engines stopped. A little breeze sighed on my cheek. I started to walk the length of the deck toward the forecastle, hugging the rail as I was still unaccustomed to a tilting deck and had not yet gained my sea legs.

I do not know what made me turn, for I had heard no sound.

I stood there looking round, suddenly fearful, my eyes the only moving parts of my body. It seemed that a change had come over the night, the ship. The shapes of familiar things, the coils of rope, gear, the bollards and such, crouching, hostile and sneering in the shadows. Then from behind me I heard footsteps, slow, dragging a little. I wheeled about. There was no one.

"Hello there!" I called.

Nothing. No answer.

I was wondering if I was beginning to hear things in addition to seeing them when a white luminescence suddenly appeared, moving out from the shadow of a life boat. My eyes started from my head. Ah Ching's ghost?

No, of course not, I thought, gritting my teeth, forcing myself to reasonableness. It was a thing called St. Elmo's fire. I had read all about it in a book of seafaring phenomena Adam had brought home for me prior to our voyage. St. Elmo's fire was the popular name for the glow caused by electrical discharges. But, and then my heart shook within me, these discharges came only during thunderstorms when lightning touched the tops of the masts.

The night was calm, too calm. And here was the glow on deck.

Terror rose in me like a cold tide. Everything that had been said at the table that morning and since came back to me. I could hear Mr. Griggs' nervous mumbling and Mathilda's placid account of the man with cheek laid bare and Adam saying, "I should have known."

And there it was. There before my eyes.

"Who . . ." I breathed, my tongue thick with fear. "Who are you?"

No answer, but a hand slowly held up. A hand wearing a yellow glove. One finger began to slowly beckon.

CHAPTER FOUR

Someone screamed. Not me; I was too terrified to make a sound. The scream came again and the glow went out, leaving a blank, inky shadow. I turned and directly behind me was a young sailor, hardly more than a boy. Even in the semi-darkness I could see his blanched face, pale as the moon in the rigging.

The next instant there was the sound of running feet, voices, and we were surrounded by a babbling circle of men, Mr. Griggs foremost among them.

"What is it, Billy? What is it?" Mr. Griggs kept asking, and by the anxious concern in his voice I guessed that this was his Billy, the son who had the makings of a first-rate seaman.

"I . . . it . . . I saw . . . I saw . . ."

"What did you see?" Mr. Griggs urged.

"I saw . . . I saw the ghost." And then because the shock was over, I suppose, Billy, finding himself the center of attention, went into an exaggerated, lurid account of the "ghost," an account which would have done credit to an accomplished writer of supernatural tales. The phantom, he said, had a long pigtail and slanting eyes and a horrible toothy smile. It was wearing a yellow glove and . . .

"Ah Ching!" someone gasped. I recognized Cookie, his round face beaded with sweat. "He lose a hand in the mine."

By then others had arrived, and little startled exclamations rippled through the crowd.

"It was him," said Billy. "It was him all right."

Mr. Ralston made his way through the gathering. The boy repeated his story. I had not thought it possible, but he managed to add a few more gruesome, imaginary details, complete with dripping blood and a voice which spoke in hollow tones. "And the captain's wife saw it, too," he added, as final confirmation to veracity.

Everybody turned their eyes on me and I, suddenly conscious of my dressing gown, wanted to shrink into the deck beneath. "Is that true?" Mr. Ralston asked. His face was in shadow, but I knew he was coolly appraising me.

"I . . . I saw a light . . ." The men pressed around, eager for my version, but remembering Adam's concern as to the spread of rumor and gossip, I finished off rather lamely, "It was a . . . a sort of glow. Nothing else."

"All right," said Mr. Ralston to the assembled crowd. "Go about your business. On your way." Then turning to me, "Come along, Mrs. Hayworth, I will take you to your cabin."

We began to walk across the deck. "I did see something," I said when we were out of earshot of the others. I described the "ghost" very briefly, and very calmly I thought. "That yellow glove," I concluded. "I saw it at my window last night."

He did not say anything. We were almost to the alleyway, and still he had not spoken. His continuing silence was like a rebuff.

"You do believe me?" I asked at last.

He paused in his step. "Would you blame me if I did not? Two supposed eyewitnesses. One a boy who gives a comic opera account, another a woman, who first denies she saw anything but a light, and then changes her mind."

"I said what I did out there because I did not want to make matters worse."

"I see." There was irony and dismissal in his voice.

"You can believe what you want," I said hotly. "And please don't bother . . . I can find my own way."

There was a short silence. "As you wish, Mrs. Hayworth. Goodnight." He turned and left me.

Just then Mathilda and Bella emerged from the alleyway. "What happened?" asked Bella excitedly. She was wearing an elegant dressing gown, all feathers and ruffles, and she reeked of gin.

"Ah Ching's ghost," I said sourly.

"Where? Where?" she clutched at my arm. "I wanna see too."

"He's gone now," I said. "And he was only a figment of my imagination."

"Who? Where?"

Mathilda disengaged Bella's hand from my arm. "All the excitement is over, Bella. Can't you see Charlotte is tired?"

It was true. I had not noticed it before, but now that Mathilda mentioned it, I suddenly felt limp as wet string.

"Wouldn't it be like me to miss all the fun," Bella complained going back to her cabin.

Mathilda turned to me. "Are you sure you'll be all right?"

"I . . . wait a moment." I went down to my door and peeked in. Adam had not yet returned. "Do you mind coming in for a bit?" I asked Mathilda. Somehow I felt the need to talk to someone, someone sympathetic.

"Of course not, my dear."

Mathilda, sitting tall and straight on one of the upholstered chairs, looked even more gaunt and unprepossessing in her camel's hair robe. Yet her very homeliness seemed comforting.

"You've had a big shock," she said. "Would you like me to get the steward to bring you some tea?"

"No, no. I am all right now." And then I told her what had happened.

She did not laugh; she did not sneer, but listened with interest. "My dear," she said at the end, "you must get it into your head not to let things like that frighten you."

"It is easy to do *now* that I am not faced with that . . . whatever it was."

"What harm can a phantom do? You could walk right through and never feel a thing. The only harm is what you do to yourself."

"You were not frightened when you saw that . . . that Baker fellow?"

"No."

"But then," I pointed out, "you did not know he was a ghost until afterwards."

"Oh, I saw him again a time or two. But I wasn't scared. I was angry. The old fool kept coming back, and we were losing business on account of him. I was mad, really mad, but not scared." She tucked her robe more firmly about her legs.

I smiled. "I do not think you were ever scared of anything."

"Oh, ho! Haven't I been? I've been frightened out of my wits more than once. Having nothing but a few crusts between us and not knowing where the next meal was coming from. Scared when—when everytime I was with child I wouldn't be able to carry it, which I wasn't, scared when Roddy was gone for three months prospecting in the desert and not a word, not a sign from him. Them's real things to be scared of. But a ghost?" She shrugged.

"I feel better, much better, already."

"That's good." She leaned over and patted my hand. "See to it you stay that way."

"It's not myself so much, it's the crew. They're all stirred up now."

"Oh, they'll quiet down. They've got a job to do. Getting me to Shanghai." She gave me another reassuring pat. "By morning it will all be forgotten."

It seemed Mathilda Jackson was right. The next day the wind picked up, and the hands were busy at their tasks of hoisting sail. For the next fortnight, at least outwardly, the *Duchess* appeared to have settled into a routine. Even our mealtimes passed without incident. The Hammersmiths and Bella Kincaid, although not on what I would call amiable terms, were decently polite to one another. Perhaps this was due in large part to Adam's presence at the table. Now that the ship was running before a good wind, he had the time to join us each night at dinner. Although I noticed he still wore a faint air of preoccupation, he appeared more relaxed and managed to make interesting conversation, telling us stories of previous voyages on both Atlantic and Pacific, stories which, of course, I had heard many times before, but which I never found dull.

We put in at Lahiana, a whaling port in the Hawaiian Islands for a fresh supply of water and fruit. It was my first view of a tropical isle and I was thoroughly enchanted. The colors were so vivid, so tangible, they almost hurt: the blue of the sea and sky, the wild profusion of pink and red and yellow blossoms against a background of emerald green, the nut-brown natives in brilliantly patterned sarongs.

We stayed for two days and two nights, then on the third day, just before sunrise, we set sail on the long stretch to Shanghai. All the passengers had gone ashore during our pause in Lahiana with the exception of Sam Ching who continued to remain unheard, unseen behind his locked cabin door. He had long since been dropped as a topic of conversation and I had almost forgotten he was on board ship when we were again reminded, rather dramatically, of his presence by Mr. Griggs. He came to breakfast the day after we left Lahiana, bleary eyed, smelling of stale drink and sweat, his hands shaking so violently he could barely lift his cup.

"I seen the ghost," he said, blinking his red-rimmed eyes at us. Mathilda, Roxanne and I, early birds as usual, were the only ones present. "We shouldn't have had the Chinaman aboard carrying the ashes of a murdered man."

"You are sure you saw a ghost?" I asked. With his whiskey-soaked brain he could have seen anything.

"I did that," he said, setting his cup down unsteadily and splashing coffee into the saucer.

Mathilda asked, "You are not afraid of a ghost, are you, Mr. Griggs?" and I envied her unruffled voice as I remembered with a sudden shiver my own fear the night the yellow glove had beckoned on the deck.

"Damned right I am. It's bad luck."

"We seem to be doing fine," I pointed out. "According to my husband we are two days ahead of schedule."

"This voyage ain't over yet. You'll see. Mark my words."

Mathilda clucked her tongue. "My, my, aren't we the prophets of doom."

He gave her a sour look. "You ladies can't picture how many things can go bad at sea, let alone sailin' on a jinxed ship."

"*The Secret Duchess* is not jinxed," I retorted impatiently. "She is a fine ship."

"Once we hit rough weather, you'll see. She rides too low in the water. Them washports . . ."

"What are washports?" Mathilda asked, calmly spreading a biscuit with marmalade.

"Them's the portholes on deck to let heavy seas drain out." His lower jaw trembled as he spoke. "There are just too damned many of them."

His heavy, complaining manner irritated me. "Mr. Griggs," I said coldly, "you must have realized all that before you signed on. You and your son . . ."

"Aye, my son. A fine lad. He's dear to me and I *should* have known better. But she didn't look so bad in port. Besides no one told me about the Chinaman." He blinked gloomily into space.

Mathilda put down her knife. "You are a pessimist if I ever saw one."

"Mark my words," he said, wagging his head. "You'll see, you'll see."

The next day the clear, azure sky began to cloud over. The harried, worn look I so hated returned to Adam's face. He spoke little, and when I pressed him he muttered something about a falling barometer.

"Does that mean a storm?" I asked.

"Perhaps."

"But we can just as easily miss it?"

"Not easily, but I hope so."

We didn't. The storm hit us with a sudden blow just before dawn. The first I knew was awakening to the whistle of the wind and the sound of Roxanne crying. A quick glance showed me that Adam had not been to bed at all. I got up and was instantly pitched across the cabin by the roll of the ship. I clung to the door jamb for a moment, my heart fluttering, then, still holding to the wall, made my way to Roxanne. She was on the floor, having been tumbled out of bed, and though she was frightened, she was unhurt. I gathered her up. "Put your arms tight around my neck, darling," I instructed.

Using the walls and the nailed down furniture as a guide, I brought her into our cabin and put her on our bunk. "Hold to the rail, darling. That's a good girl."

"What is it, Mama?" She looked up at me with enormous eyes.

"A bit of rough weather," I said, willing my voice to a casualness I was far from feeling.

I looked through the porthole, and what I saw was enough to make an already thumping heart lurch. The seas were mountainous, surging, whitecapped, foaming like milk brought to a boil. The sky, a dirty, greasy, sullen gray, was so close I could touch it with my hand.

"It's like riding a bobsled," I said with a bright smile, a smile which did not fool Roxanne, for she continued to gaze at me out of fearful eyes. "Shall we get dressed?"

Somehow, like an acrobat walking a swinging wire, I got Roxanne and myself into our clothes.

Although I was not hungry—in fact my stomach was rather queasy—it never occurred to me not to go in for breakfast. I suppose it is a British trait, sticking to routine no matter what—high tea in the jungles of Malaysia—full dress at dinner in steaming Africa—but there is something very reassuring about ritual, a defense against a strange and perhaps fearful world. And the world was fearful that morning, with the elements gone wild and the ship bucking under our feet, rocking and swaying. Bundling Roxanne and myself in oilskins, we staggered through the wet tempest into the saloon.

Mathilda Jackson was there, clinging to the table, smiling, her blue eyes serene. "This ought to make Griggs happy," she said.

I sat down, holding Roxanne on my lap. "If it does, he will be the only one."

Billy, Griggs' son, came in and he looked far from happy. His face was whiter than the cloth on the table. "The steward's come down with fever," he said. "So I am to serve in his place." His oilskins dripped, making little puddles on the floor.

"Good," said Mathilda. "What do you have for us?"

"There'll be no hot food, ma'am. The seas keep washing the galley fire out. Cookie says he's sorry." He brought out a basket from beneath his oilskins. It contained a jug, some crockery and a wrapped packet. "There's biscuits and cold tea."

We each held our cups while he managed to pour out the tea. It was strong and bitter, yesterday's tea, and the biscuits which he passed around were damp. I was somewhat surprised to find they tasted good.

"Thank you, Billy," I said. "This is a fine breakfast."

He gave me a wan smile. "Don't know when we can have a better one. The washports . . ."

"Ah," said Mathilda. "The washports again."

"They're not emptying and there's tons of water sweeping the gear away."

"It was brave of you then," I said, "to venture across deck with our food."

"Thank you, ma'am."

I was having another biscuit when the door opened. It was Ralston. He stood for a moment watching us.

"Well, I must commend you ladies," he said. "I didn't think to see anyone here."

"Never miss a meal, if I can help it," said Mathilda.

"Good sailors," he said and his eyes met mine for the briefest of moments. I could not tell whether there was surprise or approval in them. Either was as good as a compliment from Mr. Ralston. Or was it a matter of "just plain fact?"

"Will it last the day?" Mathilda asked.

"I'm afraid so," said Ralston. He drank his tea standing up, leaning against the wall for support.

Mathilda chattered away. The ship's movements seemed to become more erratic, rolling back and forth at steeper and steeper angles. The biscuits sat like a lump of sour dough under my heart. I had the awful feeling that I might be sick. Still holding Roxanne, who had grown incredibly heavy, I staggered to my feet. "If you will excuse me . . . ," I mumbled. The biscuits had risen to my throat.

Hanging on to the table, I edged myself toward the door.

Suddenly the ship lurched over and we would have fallen had not Ralston hooked his arm about us. We hung there, almost horizontally, while my heart and those rebellious biscuits struggled together in a churning sea of their own.

Then slowly the ship righted itself. Ralston's arm was still about my waist. For a moment I felt the tight muscles beneath the oilskins, and the power of the man enveloped me in a rather disturbing and frightening way. Again his eyes met mine. He dropped his arm. "I suggest you and Mrs. Jackson help one another to your respective cabins. I am wanted aft." And he ducked out the door.

Mathilda took Roxanne from me, and as we climbed the short flight of steps to the deck, the wet wind howled down to meet us. It was only a few yards from the top of the staircase to the alleyway, yet it seemed as if we were wading through miles of flood water with the rain lashing at our faces. When we reached the cabin we were thoroughly soaked.

Mathilda offered to stay with me and I accepted at once. "Please do. I would appreciate company." My stomach had commenced to quiver again. "I know Adam will not . . ."

I rushed behind the screen just in time to reach the storm basin and give up those awful biscuits. Roxanne, who had been unnaturally quiet for the past half hour, suddenly lost her ration too. She looked accusingly at me with large eyes, her face a greenish white.

"It is all right, darling. The storm will pass," I tried to assure her. Tucking her into our bed, I lashed her tightly to it while Mathilda went to her cabin for a change of clothes. When she got back we sat together beside Roxanne, clinging to the rails as the ship under us tossed about like a cork in a maelstrom. My heart grew colder and colder within me as the cracking, whipping wind tore at our tiny, unsteady island, howling with malevolent glee. Above its shriek I could hear the tumult of the seas, the noise of water pouring over the decks. I thought of the men fighting the wind and sea, grappling through the wet to keep the *Duchess* from going over. I thought of Mr. Griggs and his prophecy of bad luck and of Billy and Mr. Ralston. Most of all I thought of Adam up on the poop deck, carrying the weight of us all on his shoulders.

"It wouldn't be half bad, if we could *do* something," Mathilda said, voicing my own feelings. "It's sitting here and waiting that wears on the nerves."

"I wonder how the others are getting on?" I said.

"I can make a good guess. If I had a peephole through them walls I'd see Bella out, flat drunk, and the Hammersmiths down on their knees praying."

"Maybe that is what we should be doing, praying."

"I have been," said Mathilda. "Not on my knees, but praying."

It came to noon and past. Luncheon was not mentioned. Roxanne had brightened a little and I propped her up on the pillows and read to her from *Grimm's Fairy Tales*. Outside there was no let up, no pause, not a breathing spell for as much as half a minute in that terrible storm. At one point I found myself reading the same sentence over and over, my mind and ears preoccupied with the roar of the tempest. Ordinarily Roxanne would have caught the repetition, for she knew every word of those stories by heart, but she, too, was listening to the wind. Poor darling. Our beautiful, romantic voyage turned into a nightmare.

At about two o'clock, Mr. Hammersmith came to the door. He was clean shaven, dressed, looking none the worse for wear, but his wife, he said, was quite seasick. "Not frightened, you understand. She knows—we both do—the good Lord will pull us safely through."

"Amen," said Mathilda. "I do hope so."

"Is there anything I can do to help Mrs. Hammersmith?" I inquired.

"Thank you, but it is not her I am worried about. It is Sam Ching. His cabin is next to ours . . ."

"Is something wrong?"

"I don't rightly know. His trunk—at least, that's what I think it is—keeps crashing away at our walls. It bothered Edith so I went out and knocked on his door. He never answered."

"Cookie is the only one he will open the door to," I said.

"I was thinking he might be ill, or hurt with that trunk flying about," said Mr. Hammersmith. "If you had an extra set of keys perhaps we could take a look and make sure."

"I think the captain keeps a set in the chartroom." I got up on rubbery legs, and Mr. Hammersmith helped me across the alleyway.

The keys were on a ring in a glass case on the wall. The case was locked.

"We will have to wait for the captain," I said.

"I doubt we will see him until this blow is over," said Mr. Hammersmith. "In the meantime Sam Ching might need help."

"What do you suggest we do?" I clung to a chair as the ship went into another steep angle.

"It would only take a tap on the glass . . ."

I was faced with a decision I really did not care to make. But was it such a momentous one? Had not Adam said that I ought to help with the passengers as much as I could?

"Go ahead," I said.

He took off his shoe and smashed the glass. "I'll bring the keys back in a few minutes," he said.

41

The few minutes stretched into fifteen, then into thirty, and I began to think Hammersmith had been right. Sam Ching had either taken ill or was badly hurt. I felt a creeping sense of shame, for even in my own misery I had managed to spare a few thoughts for others, yet completely forgot the little man in his lonely isolation.

I was wondering if I should not go down to see for myself when Hammersmith tapped on the door. "None of these keys fit," he said.

"Are you sure?" I asked.

"Yes. The duplicate of mine is here. I tried the one for your door, Mrs. Jackson, and it's here too. The Chinaman's key is missing."

"Here," said Mathilda. "Let me have a go at it." She took the keys from him and went out, rolling like a true sailor with the ship.

In less than no time she was back. "You are right," she said. "The key is missing. But I don't think you have to worry about Sam Ching. He's fine."

"How do you know?" I asked.

"When the keys didn't work, I tried an old trick, a hairpin. I got the lock open all right, but he'd bolted the door from the inside. I started to rattle the door and he yelled. 'Go 'way. Go 'way.' 'Are you all right?' I asked. 'Leave me 'lone,' he hollered."

"Thank goodness for that," I breathed.

Again we sat and waited. It was getting on to four o'clock, and I noticed Mathilda had become fidgety, fussing with the brooch at her neck, tapping her feet on the floor. Finally she got up. "I'll be back. I'm going to take a peek and see what's happening."

"Mathilda, you cannot go out on deck," I said, horrified.

"I won't go all the way. Just a quick look."

She was back in a short while. "It's truly hell out there," she said. "They're at the pumps."

All I could think was the *Duchess* had sprung a leak. "Ought we to put on our life jackets?" I asked, frightened out of my wits.

"I suppose," she said calmly, apparently much refreshed by her little excursion, "the captain will let us know when we need them."

"Yes . . . yes." She had faith in Adam, the kind of faith I should have, I scolded myself. But my teeth continued to chatter and the warm cloak I had wrapped myself in was no protection against the chill in my bones.

The ship went on tossing and pitching. She rolled and groaned, standing on one end, then the other, until I was sure that the next moment or the next she would break apart, spewing us into the roiling sea.

It got dark. When I glanced through the porthole I could not see the sky or the sea anymore. Mathilda, staggering to her feet, lit the lamp. It sputtered and flickered and swung, casting our leaping shadows on the walls. The roar of the wind and water went on. I forgot the time, the hour, the day, forgot why I had ever wanted to leave shore, the comfort of our little house on Beacon Street. Everything was insanity now, without rhyme or reason. Only a world of wind and water.

Somehow the night passed, and when dawn came it seemed the fury of the storm had abated. Either that or I had become so numbed it no longer mattered. Mathilda had fallen asleep, her long chin resting on her thin breast. I envied her for I had not closed my eyes once. An hour later Adam came in, his face haggard, grooved in deep lines.

"Are they still pumping?" I asked.

He must have caught a tremor in my voice. He replied crossly, "They are. A little pumping does not mean a sinking ship."

Mathilda, awake now, got to her feet. "I'll be going."

Adam was instantly apologetic. "Please don't leave, Mrs. Jackson. I hope you forgive my sharpness, but I've had a hellish night."

"Certainly," said Mathilda. "I understand."

"I've just come in for some dry clothes. I'll change in the chartroom."

I got him his clothes. He kissed Roxanne, then me, and was gone.

"Do you think we should try for breakfast?" Mathilda asked.

"Breakfast!" I exclaimed and we both laughed. "If Cookie could not get the fire going yesterday, he most certainly will not be able to today."

"It's biscuits and cold tea, then," said Mathilda stoically. "I've had worse. Are you coming?"

"Why . . . I suppose so," I said.

The saloon was empty. We sat down at the table, a little damp but, having survived the awful night, in rather good spirits.

"I could drink a gallon of coffee," said Mathilda. "The kind that's boiled and brewed over an open fire. And bacon and homemade biscuits. Did I ever tell you how wonderful bacon smells cooking in a pan on a frosty morning with the sun just coming over a mountain range?"

I gave her a weak smile. The breakfast did not appeal to me, but the dawn coming over the mountains did.

Suddenly there was a lull in the wind and I heard the jangling of bells, a shout, "Man overboard!"

Mathilda and I looked at each other. And then I was on my feet, dragging Roxanne out the door and up the stairs. There were men swarming on the deck where the seas were still coming over the rail.

The ship suddenly lurched, shivered and shuddered, turning as it was brought up. The men worked frantically at a life boat.

"I'm going to see who it is," I said. "Will you watch Roxanne?"

"I'll go," offered Mathilda. "I got steadier legs than you." And she was out on deck before I could protest.

I made my way to the passage and went into the chartroom where the porthole there had a better view. It could not be Adam, I thought. It must not be.

They had got the life boat over. Several men, Griggs among them, clambered over the rail. The little boat seemed a futile thing, rising and falling in the big seas. There was no sign of the man who had fallen overboard. The boat pulled away, and at any moment I expected to see it capsize as it slid and rose, slid and rose up and down the huge, great troughs of water. Brave men. I took back every nasty thought I had ever had of Griggs.

Mathilda found me in the chartroom, my face still glued to the porthole.

"It's Billy," she said. "Griggs' boy. He was on his way with our breakfast when a big wave caught him."

I felt wretched. "They will find him," I said. "Adam told me once of a man going overboard in a storm who was rescued."

But though they searched through the morning and on into the afternoon, they did not find him, and he was never seen again.

CHAPTER FIVE

One would think that the sole purpose of that fiendish storm was to snatch Billy Griggs from us, for that very afternoon the wind ceased and by nightfall the sky cleared into a brilliantly hued sunset.

The steward, even more sallow of face and still shaky from his bout of fever, served our dinner. Except for Griggs, we were all there. Though it was our first hot meal in two days and the ship had come through without major damage, Billy's loss threw a pall of gloom over the assemblage. Adam sat with a little frown between his eyes, making no effort at conversation as he had done so many times before. I could guess his feelings. The loss of anyone on board, crew or passenger, was his responsibility.

Bella frowned, too, and was mostly silent. But I think her lack of speech was mainly due to the aftereffects of drinking. She remembered hardly any of the storm, she said, having consumed half a bottle of gin when the wind first began to blow, and the other half during the night. Thomas Hammersmith upon hearing this gave her a derisive, scornful look and puckered up his lips, but he said nothing. It was all to the good. I do not think I could have borne a sermon or sharp words at the tag end of everything else.

The sharp words did come, however, later in our cabin, and from Adam. He had discovered the broken case in the chartroom. When I explained what had happened, our concern for Sam Ching, it was like adding fuel to the fire. "What right had you to give those keys to anyone?" he demanded of me.

"I . . . why . . . I thought under the circumstances . . ."

"There are no circumstances!" he thundered in a voice which I was sure could be heard in the forecastle. Adam and I had had our little differences, our quarrels in the past, but never had I seen him so enraged and it was a frightening thing. He was like a stranger.

"Adam . . . I did not know . . ."

"You should have had more sense. The chartroom is forbidden territory. I cannot have everyone and anyone . . ."

"I am not everyone and anyone!" I bit back. I did not have titian hair for nothing. And my temper, more easily aroused than Adam's, had far more practice. "One moment you ask me to try and share responsibility for the passengers, and when an emergency comes up . . ."

"What emergency?"

"I told you. Mr. Hammersmith . . ."

"Mr. Hammersmith ought to mind his own business."

"He was only trying to help."

"Sam Ching does not want his help." And with that he slammed out the door.

I had forgotten to tell him Sam Ching's key was missing, but at that point I was sick of the whole matter.

I fell asleep weeping silently into my pillow that night. I do not know when Adam came to bed, but when I awoke in the morning he was there beside me. It was the first night I could ever remember when, sharing the same bed, I had not slept in Adam's arms. I pushed myself up on an elbow and stared down at his face, his forehead frowning even in sleep.

He opened his eyes. "Charlotte?"

I put my finger to his lips. "Adam, let us not quarrel anymore. I don't want us to be this way."

"I said some rather hasty things, didn't I?"

"Yes . . . yes, you did."

"Flying off the handle." He reached up for me. "Give me a kiss and let's be friends again."

So we patched up our quarrel. Yet in the days that followed there remained a distance between us. I could feel it in his absent touch, in the way he spoke to me, and in his long, withdrawn silences. He was like a man completely absorbed in another world. It was the ship, I told myself, *The Secret Duchess*. And gradually as time went by the *Duchess* began to take on the essence of a living entity, appearing in my thoughts much as another woman might have done, mysterious, possessive—my rival.

I wondered, too, why Adam had been so put out with me for trying to assist Hammersmith. It was obvious he had resented the invasion of Sam Ching's privacy as much as he had the breaking into of the key case in the chartroom. And I could not understand, no matter how I thought on it, why Adam should feel so protective of that unknown little man.

I did not dwell on the matter for long. Again, we had a diversion which drove Sam Ching from my mind. It was Mr.

Griggs. Ever since Billy had been lost in the sea, the second mate had let himself go completely, appearing at the table unshaven, muttering incoherently, and more often than not, thoroughly drunk. I thought him rather pitiful, and in a sense I could sympathize with his grief, having come so close to losing my own child at one time. But Adam had a ship to run, and he had no choice but to order Mr. Griggs confined to his cabin. The second mate did not go willingly. I heard his loud, profane protest in the alleyway (his cabin was opposite Sam Ching's) as did the other passengers, and quite possibly the whole ship. Mr. Ralston had been given the unpleasant task of carrying out Adam's orders, and that seemed to be one of Mr. Griggs' chief complaints.

"I won't take orders from you!" Mr. Griggs shouted. "If the cap'n wants me to stay put, then let him say so hisself."

"Mr. Griggs, don't argue," I heard Ralston say. "When you sober up, you can come out."

"Sober up, huh! I *am* sober, sober as a judge. And I ain't . . ."

There was the sound of a scuffle and then the banging of a door.

Naturally, it followed that Mr. Griggs should be the main topic of conversation at dinner that night. It all started innocently enough with Bella defending the second mate. "He has a right to drink, if he wants," she said. "The poor man. It keeps him going."

Mr. Hammersmith turned rigid. "Drink is evil. The work of the Devil. Mr. Griggs would do better to ask the Lord to carry him through his time of trial. And . . ." He leaned across the table and pointed to her glass of wine. ". . . I would advise you to do the same."

"I don't need your advice."

"You not only need it, you need guidance as well."

"Well, I'll be damned," said Bella, and she threw the contents of her wine glass in his face.

There was a momentary stunned silence. Then Mr. Ralston got to his feet, a look of disgust in his eyes, and without a word, left the saloon.

"I don't think that was necessary," said Adam, very controlled. "Now Mrs. Kincaid, I am sure if you and Mr. Hammersmith . . ."

But it was like trying to pour oil on very troubled waters. Bella began to shout obscenities, disjointed phrases, something about "damaged goods," and "Edith, the bitch." I did not see what she had against Edith, since the girl never uttered a word at table, except for "pass the butter," or "may I have the salt?" At any rate, I was glad Roxanne was safely tucked in bed, for Bella's language—a good deal of which I did not understand myself—would have done credit to a drover with a recalcitrant mule.

Mr. Hammersmith, having dabbed the wine from his face with a napkin, waited for a lull in Bella's tirade. "I turn the other cheek," he said when it finally came, "because I am a good Christian. My advice—whether you want it or not— is to repent before it is too late." He took his wife by the arm and, with stiff dignity, went out the door, Bella shouting after him, "Wait! Wait! I have something to tell you that'll open your ears . . ."

I saw Adam's fist clenched tightly around a fork, and I had the feeling he was as close to striking a woman as he had ever been in his life.

"Charlotte," he said in a voice which cut across Bella's, "I think Mrs. Kincaid would appreciate your escorting her to her cabin."

Bella, her cheeks flaming beneath the powder and paint, gave Adam a withering look which he returned with his most charming smile. "We all have our bad days, Mrs. Kincaid. If you require anything in your cabin, the steward will be glad to serve you."

I got to my feet, not certain if Bella would come, or turn her fury on me.

Adam kept on smiling, and gradually Bella's flush faded. She leaned forward and touched his sleeve. "Are those your orders, Captain?"

"I never give orders to a lady," he said gallantly, "just suggestions."

She rose and took my arm. "Good night, then."

She was heavy and had a tendency to sway, but we made it up the stairs and to her cabin without mishap. "I hate to get all riled up that way," she said. "Besides being bad for the complexion, it gives everyone the wrong impression. I'm really very easy to get along with, don't you think?"

I searched in my mind for some suitable reply, and finding none, remained silent.

"Come in," she invited. "Sit for a few minutes."

"Roxanne . . ."

"Oh, Roxanne is all right. Come in."

To say the cabin was untidy would be an understatement. It appeared that Bella had never learned the purpose of cupboards or bureau drawers, for her clothing, petticoats, dresses, and chemises were strewn haphazardly on the chair, on the bunk, on the floor. The dressing table was littered with a profusion of scent bottles, dirty mugs, stockings and gin bottles. Bella cleared a chair, bundling the clothing together and shoving it under a pillow. "Have a seat," she offered. Then going to the dressing table she unstoppered a gin bottle. "Would you like a nip?"

"No, thank you."

She poured some gin into a mug. "Helps the digestion." She drank. "And settles the stomach."

She sat down opposite me on the bunk. "Seeing as you're the captain's wife I think I ought to explain something."

"It is not necessary," I said, feeling rather uncomfortable and wondering how soon I could decently leave.

"Hell, it ain't," she said. "I don't want the captain's bad opinion. Or yours either when it comes to it."

"We all lose our tempers at times. Mr. Hammersmith can be quite dogmatic."

"Mr. Hammersmith is a pious humbug."

"Why, I suppose he means well," I said cautiously, not wanting to rouse Bella again, or malign Mr. Hammersmith.

"He can mean well to someone else. Not me. I've been pretty much the lady until now, keeping my mouth shut. But he's gone too far, and I don't give a damn if the whole ship knows about it."

"About Mr. Hammersmith?" I asked.

"His wife, to be exact." She took another drink.

"You knew Edith Hammersmith?" I asked, recalling the two women's first meeting and the swift look of surprise which had passed between them.

"Did I ever!" She began to laugh, hearty raucous laughter and, in its coarse way, it was rather infectious.

I smiled at her.

"You know, I got a confession to make."

"Oh?"

"I'm not an opera singer."

I lifted my brows, feigning surprise.

"Well, I thought you might have read about me in the papers. You don't know who I am?"

"I'm not much for reading the papers," I said, avoiding a direct answer.

"I can sing, but most of my singing was done in my parlor. And it wasn't opera. Pass the bottle, will you, that's a good girl."

I did as she asked.

"Well, then . . ." She took another long drink. "I'm a parlor house madam. There it is. Out in the open. I don't care anymore about its being a secret. Respectability smells to high heaven. But it ain't my point to give my opinions on respectability. What I want to say . . . the plain truth is, Edith ain't no more a missionary than I'm an opera singer. She was one of my girls when I had my place up at Rainbow Creek."

"Edith?" I asked incredulously. I could no more picture pale Edith with her childlike bony wrists as a demimonde than I could a plucked sparrow.

"Yes, Edith. She was with me about eight months and then she left. That was some two years ago. I don't know where she went; I never bothered to ask. None of the girls stay for long. They get the wanderlust, you know. They come and they go. But I remember their faces and most of their names, and I remember Edith."

"I wonder if her husband knows."

"He doesn't," a voice said, and we turned our heads.

The door had opened and Edith Hammersmith was standing there.

"Aren't you the sly one," said Bella. "Listening at the keyhole."

Edith came in and softly shut the door behind her. "I had a good idea, Bella," she said, "that you'd be up to something sooner or later."

"Did you, now?" said Bella, sloshing the gin in her mug.

"Yes, I know you well enough. Pretending to be an opera singer . . ."

"It's as good as pretending to be a missionary's wife."

"I *am* a missionary's wife," she said, drawing herself up. "When I left Rainbow Creek, I never went back to that life again."

"That's what they all say," said Bella, lifting the mug to her lips. "I haven't known a girl yet who doesn't swear she is—or is going to—walk the straight and narrow."

"I did. I do," said Edith, her voice low and intense. "When I met Thomas I had been working for a year and a half as laundress and maid for a Mrs. Blackstone in San Francisco. I met him at one of those tent revival meetings, and I saw the light and came to the Lord through him."

"Oh, for heaven's sake," Bella said. "Pass the bottle, Charlotte."

"It's the truth," Edith said. "And Thomas courted me like

a gentleman. When he asked me to marry him and share his work, I was the happiest girl alive."

"And you didn't tell him?" Bella said. "You didn't give him the chance to rescue you from a life of sin?"

"He knows nothing of that. Nothing." The color flooded Edith's face and her eyes widened. "And I think you had better not tell him."

Bella laughed.

I said, "Mrs. Hammersmith—Edith, do you think it a good idea to keep this—this past of yours from your husband?"

"I don't want him to know," she said stubbornly.

"But surely if he is the Christian he professes to be . . ."

"I don't want him to know."

Bella snorted. "I'll tell you one thing, Edith, my girl. If he says another insulting word to me, I'll give him a mouthful."

"You do," said Edith coldly, "and you will be sorry. Very sorry."

"And what is that supposed to mean?"

Edith came up to Bella and slowly drew a long knife from her sleeve. The silver blue blade glimmered in the lamplight. "Do you see this, *Madam* Kincaid?" She touched the point to Bella's ample bosom. "I will kill you if you breathe one word." Under her rouged cheeks Bella blanched.

"Edith!" I said, shocked. I did not think she could possibly be serious. Such a small creature. It was as if a mouse had suddenly threatened a tiger. "You do not know what you are saying."

"Don't I?" she turned to me, shoving the knife under my chin. I felt its sharp point tickling my throat. "The same goes for you. I'll kill you both if Thomas ever finds out."

"I . . ." My eyes turned downward to the shimmering blade. It had a thick, carved wooden handle, not a dainty weapon by anyone's standards. "I—I shall never tell him, of course. But the knife . . ."

"The knife is mine. It was given to me by my Papa. 'Keep it,' he told me. 'You might find it handy.' And if Bella remembers, I know how to use it."

Bella gasped. "I clean forgot!"

"Don't forget," said Edith. "Well, do I get a promise from you both?"

"I promise," said Bella.

"That means no one, not the captain, no one is to know."

"Yes," I said.

"All right, all right," said Bella. "Just put that bloody thing away."

Edith slipped the knife back into her sleeve and, going to the door, said, "Good night, ladies," in a soft, demure voice.

Bella took a long drink.

"Do you think she really meant it?" I asked, still aghast.

"Oh, she meant it. It had slipped my mind altogether. I can remember their names and their faces good enough, but sometimes I get mixed up as to who did what. I should have reremembered *her,* a cat when she's crossed. And she did kill a man with that knife."

"She what?"

"Put it right through him. It was self-defense—that's what *she* claimed. Said he was beating her."

"Did you believe it?"

She shrugged. "I had no choice. I didn't want to give my place a bad name. The sheriff was a friend and we fixed it up between us."

"But that was . . ."

"Murder?" She reached for the bottle. "Yes. And I guess you could say she got away with it."

CHAPTER SIX

That Bella Kincaid had been a parlor house madam had shocked me, but, on reflection, not unduly so. Her appearance, the powder, the dangling earrings, the boisterous, coarse manner all fitted in with my conception of such a role. But wide-eyed, shy Edith Hammersmith as a scarlet woman was still incomprehensible. I would have never believed her disreputable past had I not heard her admit it, nor have believed the violence which lay beneath those wide violet eyes had I not felt the point of her knife. Her threat to kill Bella and me if we divulged her secret was rather theatrical (and in my case, at least, unnecessary), but frightening nevertheless, and it reminded me again that people were often far different than they seemed by outward appearance. It was a reminder that would nag at me again and again when, in a short while, suspicion and mistrust would color my view of our little world.

Bella stayed away from the dining saloon for two days, and when she returned for her noon meal on the third, no reference was made to her quarrel with the Hammersmiths or to her rude behavior. Bella was much subdued and Mr. Hammersmith, I noticed, preached less. Perhaps this was partly due to his obtaining Adam's permission to hold services for the crew and passengers each Sunday morning, where for an hour and a half he could exhort in the Lord's name to his heart's content. At any rate he confined his speech at the table to the weather and to little anecdotes of his travels among the mining towns of the West. Once he spoke of Rainbow Creek, and I had an anxious moment or two, glancing quickly at Edith and Bella. Neither gave any sign of having heard of such a place, although Mathilda remarked she and Roddy had passed through there more than once on their journeys.

To my relief Hammersmith did not dwell on Rainbow Creek but passed on to talk of his coming work in China. "Our mission at home is a poor one," he said, "and Edith and I will be hard put to carry out some of our plans. We would like to build a church, a small one, of course, and a school. But I have great faith the money will come from somewhere. The Lord in his good time, will see to it."

Whatever the Lord had in store for Thomas Hammersmith, He, for the time being, had decreed another calm for the *Duchess*. Once again the sails were furled and the engines called into action, pumping us steadily across a sea smooth as glass. With the sun, bright as a new penny, shining benignly down upon us, I sensed a general air of well-being aboard ship. Adam, though a little concerned by our limited supply of coal, was pleased at the ship's performance. Mr. Griggs, pale and rather trembly, but fully sobered, had been allowed to take up his duties again. And the crew seemed to step and move about in a lively manner, having, I suppose, been "kicked into shape."

"You see," said Mathilda to me one afternoon as we sat side by side on deck chairs, "our troubles are all behind us. I'm willing to wager nothing but a happy voyage lies ahead."

I wish that Mathilda had been as good at prophecy as Griggs had been. But she was not.

Early Friday morning I was awakened rudely by the sound of the clanging bells which I had not heard since Billy's disappearance. Adam was out of the bunk and half dressed before I could find my voice. "What is it?" I asked.

"I don't know," he answered, pulling on his boots. "It can be anything."

With nervous hands I got into my clothes and, because Roxanne would not be left behind, I had to hurriedly dress her too. By the time we got down to the deck all I could see was a group of men at one of the hatches, a thin column of smoke rising above their heads.

Mathilda was standing on the outer edge. "A fire in the hold," she said to me as I came up.

"A fire?" Craning my neck I saw Adam and Ralston directing the men who were hosing water into the hatch. There was a hissing sound followed by little puffs of white steam.

"I think we have it," I heard Ralston say. "Mr. Phipps, would you go down and have a look?"

Mr. Phipps, the bosun, a bandy-legged man with a face brown and wrinkled as a walnut, disappeared into the hatch and a few minutes later reappeared, coughing. "The fire's out, sir," he said to Adam. "But . . ."

"Any damage?" Adam asked.

"No . . . not much from the fire that I could see. A couple charred boxes. But, sir, it appears some of them boxes has been opened. The ones with the furs."

"Let me have a look," said Adam.

Five minutes went by, ten. The engines throbbed and chugged on. The early sun, flooding the sea with a sapphire polish, climbed a notch higher. The men began to shuffle and mumble among themselves. "Spontaneous combustion," I heard someone say. "No," replied another. "That's only when you're carrying coal." "Wrong," said another. "There ain't enough ventilation."

When Adam finally emerged from the hold his face was grim. "Someone has been down there with an axe and destroyed several crates of furs."

My heart constricted. The furs meant for China were a valuable part of our cargo.

"I want all hands, except for the helmsman, on deck," said Adam.

Since most of the men were already there it took only a matter of minutes to round up the others. Adam explained what had happened. "A fire and wrecked cargo. Someone was responsible. Now who?"

There was a long silence, the men's faces stony, without expression.

"All right, if the guilty party will not own up, then I want to know who saw him. Who saw anyone go into the hatch?"

There was a murmur, exchanged glances, but no one spoke out.

"Who had the deck watch?" Adam asked.

"Coles, here." A man stepped forward. He was fairly young with a great mass of straw colored hair.

"You did not see anything?"

"No, sir."

Adam stared at him for the space of ten seconds. "That is rather hard to believe. If you were at your proper station you must have had a good view of the deck."

Coles remained silent.

"I have no alternative but to confine you to quarters, Coles."

Coles made his way through the crowd, a sullen look on his face.

"Again I ask," said Adam, "is there anyone among you who saw the guilty party?"

There was a general shaking of heads. "Maybe it was Ah Ching's ghost," someone said, and the others tittered nervously.

"I want no lip," said Adam, in a hard, angry voice. "This is a serious matter. You could have all been fried in your bunks. All right then, I shall have to set up a double watch. The loss of a little sleep might refresh your memories."

The men dispersed and I went up to Adam. "Not now, Charlotte," he said impatiently and went striding toward the upper deck.

To my consternation and embarrassment Mr. Ralston was standing a few feet away. I was certain he had seen the little exchange between Adam and me, although not a muscle of his handsome features betrayed it. Nevertheless, I could well guess what he was thinking. The captain's wife meddles and her husband is not at all happy she is here. It angered me that he should seem so superior.

"And what do you think, Mr. Ralston?" I asked. "Have you any ideas on the subject?"

"It could have been anyone," he said.

"But why should a man . . ."

"Or woman," he interposed.

"A woman?"

"Why not? A woman is as capable of mischief as a man."

"You really do despise women, don't you?" I said.

"It is not that I despise them, Mrs. Hayworth, I simply do not trust them." His gaze rested on me briefly, then moved to the distant horizon.

A strange man, very strange, I thought. Curiosity impelled me to ask, "Are you married, Mr. Ralston?"

His eyes came back, fixing on mine, intense, piercing, glittering. "I was—once. She is dead." And without another word, he turned and walked away.

His look, his cold voice, his abrupt departure seemed to be in the nature of an accusation. And I wondered what sort of woman he had been married to, and if she were responsible for this burning dislike of all females.

Ralston's implied snub, coming on the heels of Adam's real one, bruised my feelings. I sat in my cabin all morning, feeling very unhappy with the world and with men of the sea in particular, until Adam, finding me there, apologized for his curt behavior. Looking at his worried eyes, I felt rather ashamed, a shallow fool, for having considered my touchy pride above his latest trouble.

"Have you found the person who started the fire?" I asked him.

He had removed his jacket and shirt and was shaving at the mirror. "No. There are several it would be easy to suspect, I suppose, but I need definite proof. Starting a fire at sea is a serious crime."

"Could it have been an accident?"

I watched his face in the mirror, his brows furrowed over the bridge of his nose. "I have thought of that. A careless match tossed down the ventilator, a spark from the galley stove. But the slashed crates—that was no accident."

"Perhaps the furs were destroyed by someone before the fire."

"Perhaps, but I am inclined to believe the two went together. And I cannot have this sort of deliberate vandalism going on."

"Mr. Ralston," I said, "is of the opinion it could have just as easily been a woman."

He smiled. It was the first time Adam had smiled in so long I secretly forgave Ralston his outrageous statement.

"He also tells me he does not trust women." I picked up Adam's jacket and began brushing the lint from it.

"If he says so, I suppose it is true."

I picked a stubborn thread from the collar. "Did you know he had been married?"

"You had quite a confidential little talk, I see."

"No—not actually. I just came out point blank and asked him. That is all."

He got his shirt from the chair and put it on.

"I wonder," I mused aloud, "what she was like."

"Who was like?"

"His wife. I would guess she is the cause of his bitterness."

"Mr. Ralston intrigues you, does he?"

"Yes. All mysteries intrigue me."

He took the jacket from me. "I wonder why women are always drawn to mysterious, handsome men, especially those who are professed woman haters."

"Adam, I said nothing about being drawn to him. He puzzles me."

"He is a challenge and you love challenges."

"You are not thinking . . ."

"I am not thinking you have fallen madly in love with him. No. But what I am thinking is how your mind is working. Ah, you say to yourself, so he hates women. I will show him what a fine, good woman is like."

I felt the heat rush to my face, he was that close to the truth.

"Never mind," said Adam, kissing the top of my head. "I doubt our good Mr. Ralston will be impressed. I have a feeling that you are not the first woman who has tried to change his mind."

"Adam, if you are hinting I am a flirt . . ."

"Who? Me? Never!"

"You are making mock of me. If you have the slightest notion I am trying to entice Mr. Ralston, I shall never speak to the man again."

He sighed. "Charlotte, please. Let us not quarrel over Mr. Ralston." Saying that, he gave me a perfunctory kiss on the cheek and left.

It was late, well past two in the morning, and I was reading by lamplight, waiting for Adam. I had developed a curious, inexplicable insomnia, a condition I had never suffered from before. The others claimed the sea air was like a soporific and, once their heads hit the pillow, only a screaming alarm could awaken them. And Bella, of course, had her gin. But there was something inside me, a mystic other self, if you will, that seemed to come to life once night closed in, a waiting self, uneasy, anxious, holding its breath. And the oddest thing of all was that Adam's presence, even when he was close to me, touching me, did not dispel, did not vanquish, this other, persistent me. In the deathwatch hours of the night I would remember the yellow glove at my window, the mysterious glow I had seen on deck. I would speculate on Ah Ching, think of his ashes resting uneasily among us, and I would begin to believe *The Secret Duchess* was truly haunted. I can recall how I argued, struggled, fought with myself in an attempt to bring my thoughts back from ghosts and hauntings and the unexplainable things which had happened and could happen again.

I was sitting thus when I caught the sound of a dull thump outside the door. Such was my state of mind, the thump, not a particularly frightening sound under ordinary circumstances, bolted me out of bed as if I had been jabbed by a hat pin, a wild fear prickling my skin. I stood in the middle of the room, a hand on my quivering mouth, my imagination rampant with visions of yellow, disembodied fingers blindly groping from door to door. I listened, tense, waiting. In the distance I heard the chug-chugging of the engines, steady, a counterpart to my own beating heart. Finally I forced myself to the door and opening it cautiously, I saw a man, his arms flung out, sprawled full length on the floor. It was Ralston.

So much for my foolish fancies, I thought, ashamed, as I knelt quickly and felt of his pulse. It beat erratically under my fingers. He was so still, his face tinged with such a ghastly pallor, I would have thought him dead were it not for that faintly throbbing pulse. He must have had a seizure of some sort was my thought.

I could not leave him lying there. Not wanting to wake any of the passengers, I knocked softly on Mr. Griggs' door. "Mr. Griggs," I whispered. After a few moments I heard him stirring and grumbling, and then his grizzled face appeared in the doorway. I did not have to tell him about Mr. Ralston. His eyes went to him at once. Together, Mr. Griggs bearing much of the burden, we dragged, half carried Ralston to his bunk.

"A good draught of whiskey will get him round," said Mr. Griggs. "But I have none. You know they took every last drop from me. If you would ask Cookie?" There was a hopeful look in his eye which I found disquieting.

"I have some aromatic spirits in my kit," I said. "It will do just as well. And if you will fetch Captain Hayworth, I would appreciate it."

I ran and got the kit. No sooner had I placed the little vial under Mr. Ralston's nose when his hand came up and swept it away. He opened his eyes and stared at me, his bewilderment slowly changing to hostility.

"I found you unconscious in the alleyway," I said. "You must have fainted."

"Fainted?" he said. "I have never fainted in my life. Someone hit me." He tried to lift himself, then, clenching his jaw, sank back onto the pillows.

"Where?"

"On the back of the head," he said, feeling of it gingerly.

"Let me see."

He gave me a defiant look, but nevertheless turned his head. There was a lump big as a robin's egg.

"Some cold compresses will get it down," I said.

I found a pitcher of water behind the screen. The water was tepid, not cold, but it would have to do. I wet a towel and brought it to Mr. Ralston, placing it on his injured head. "Mr. Griggs has gone to fetch the captain," I said. "But in the meanwhile I think I will go down and ask Cookie if he can spare some flour and mustard for a poultice."

"I strongly advise against walking about the ship in the dark," he said.

I do not think it had occurred to me until that moment the frightening implication of Mr. Ralston's injury. Someone had assaulted him, someone who, even now, might be waiting, hiding in the shadows. "Did you see . . . ?"

"No. If I had I would be out there, smashed head or no, wringing his neck."

"I cannot understand it, any of it," I said, shaking my head. "First a fire, now this assault. Poor Adam, his troubles never seem to end."

"You are fond of your husband." It was a statement not a question.

"I love him," I said simply.

"Love." He gave the word an amused, ironic twist.

"You do not believe in love, Mr. Ralston?"

"No. Love is a myth. A fickle, deceiving myth." He winced as he pushed himself up higher on the pillow.

"Yet, you must have been in love once to have married."

His feverish eyes cut through me. "You are a naive romantic."

"I suppose I am," I said hotly, the red staining my cheeks. "And you are a hardened, gloomy cynic."

"A cynic, yes. And if you had my memories you would be the same."

"I am sorry to have touched on a sensitive point. How long has it been since your wife died?"

He looked at me for a long moment. "My wife never died." He took the towel from behind his head, and suddenly flung it across the room. "If you want to know the truth, she ran off. Yes, she ran off with a miserable ship's agent in Melbourne. A silly, frivolous woman enticed by a few baubles, a new dress, a house with a white picket fence. She did not like being alone so much, she said, she did not like being married to a sailor. And I hope to God she and that man of hers burn in hell."

"I am sorry," I repeated, shocked.

"Don't be," he said. "It was good riddance. And now, if you don't mind, I would like to get some sleep. My head is throbbing."

It was a dismissal. He did not want my pity, my sympathy. I went back to the cabin thinking of Mr. Ralston and how his wife's desertion had blighted his life, his ambition, his trust of women. He was proud yes, but his pride was like vinegar, curdling his soul, and I could picture him old before his time, his handsome face set in a permanent scowl. And that would be more of a pity than his wife's death.

Well, it was not my concern. What was important, as Adam had pointed out, was Adam's dependence on him as a good, loyal officer. Now more than ever Adam needed his support, what with someone roaming the ship, setting fires and clubbing heads. And thinking of Adam I suddenly remembered that I had sent Griggs to fetch him. I was wondering why he had not come when Mr. Griggs, himself, appeared at the door.

"I couldn't find the cap'n," he said.

I rose to my feet, a sudden vision of Adam, like Ralston, lying in some passageway with a cracked head. "Have you looked?"

"From stem to stern," he said, coming into the cabin and closing the door. His eyes had a funny glazed stare, his mouth hung slack, a thread of saliva drooling from one corner of it.

I turned cold all over. "Have you tried the chartroom?"

"Yes. He's not there."

"What is it you want?" I asked. Some instinct made me move closer to Roxanne's doorway.

"He killed my Billy," he said, his eyes glittering.

"Why . . . no, Mr. Griggs. Billy was swept overboard. The captain had nothing to do with his death."

"He killed my Billy. He was the apple of my eye. Had the makin's of a fine seaman. He would have gone right to the top. Do you know that?"

"Yes, Mr. Griggs, I am sure he would have done so." I took another step backward.

"He killed him. The cap'n killed my Billy."

"No . . ."

"Don't you argue with me," he hissed.

I was terrified. The man had gone quite mad. And yet he had seemed so sane, so rational in Mr. Ralston's cabin. "Perhaps, Mr. Griggs, if you came back later and spoke to my husband."

"I ain't comin' back later. I'm out to make him pay for what he done. He and that damned first mate."

"You hit Mr. Ralston!" It was out before I could catch myself.

"Not half hard enough. He had too thick a skull. I wanted to smash . . . to smash it." He threw back his jacket and I saw a long spike stuck in the band of his trousers. He pulled it out.

"Mr. Griggs . . ."

"I'm goin' to kill you all, every last one," he muttered. He began to move toward me, his eyes popping from his head like an idiot's. "And don't you open your mouth to scream."

My mouth, with an independent will of its own, opened. I screamed.

Mr. Griggs lunged at me and missed, the spike smashing

over my head against the wall. Behind me I heard Roxanne calling. I did not dare turn my back on Griggs, but kept sliding along my hands groping for Roxanne's door. He started to come at me again and I shrank back. He raised his arm . . .

And then suddenly Adam was there and Phipps, the bosun, and Ralston with his injured head. Mr. Griggs fought like ten savages, but at last he was subdued, Adam trussing his arms and legs with a sheet from the bunk.

"I am afraid I should have seen this coming on," said Adam.

They chained Griggs to his bunk in his cabin, and there he remained until the Hammersmiths and Bella Kincaid complained of the noise he made. They took him below and locked him in a cabin 'tween decks, but even so on quiet nights we could sometimes hear him shouting, out of his mind, completely and forever mad.

CHAPTER SEVEN

In a way Mr. Griggs' final disintegration into madness came as a relief. Although he was too far gone to understand or answer any of Adam's questions, we were certain that in addition to assaulting Ralston he was the one responsible for the destroyed furs and the fire in the hold. Privately I was also convinced Mr. Griggs, his tottering mind shaken by the presence of a dead man's ashes and fixed on the notion the ship was jinxed, had masqueraded as Ah Ching's phantom. His distorted reasoning, I assumed, was to undermine the crew's morale to a point where they would refuse to sail the ship unless Adam turned back. The man had been nervous and jumpy from the start. With Billy's death, his last hold on reason had vanished.

Adam blamed himself bitterly, not for Griggs' madness, but for his own faulty perception, his failing to rightly assess Griggs' mental stability before he had signed him on. The ship was now an officer short, and there was no one qualified to take Griggs' place. He and Ralston were forced to alternate watches and take up the slack themselves, which meant that I saw less than ever of Adam.

But it was a small price to pay for the quiet, dull routine which we seemed to settle into once more. The breezes stiffened, the engines were halted and the sails blossomed. We rode with the wind, westward, day after day, having little to talk of but the weather and Cookie's fine hand with a stew. And I did not mind the boredom—I had had enough of melodrama.

For some odd reason, however, my sleeplessness still persisted. Since Griggs' incarceration I no longer feared walking on deck at night, and so I would go for a short stroll each evening around ten or eleven o'clock. I liked that time best of all. Everyone, excepting the watch, had retired and the silence, broken only by the wind and the creaking of the rigging, was restful. I would feel the moist breeze on my face and taste the sea salt on my lips and marvel at the stars, brilliant with white fire, scattered across the domed velvet sky. It was during those walks I came quite close to understanding why Adam loved the sea so much.

Then one night I made a discovery which left me a little less partial to the beauties of maritime life. I was taking my customary stroll when suddenly, looking up, I found myself gazing into two fierce, golden eyes. Unwinking, sulphurous, they burned like a steady flame, transfixing me to the spot. The next instant the eyes shifted and something soft and swift flew past me. I heard a thud, the terrified squeal of a creature in agony. Another squeal, then silence.

"Out walking, Mrs. Hayworth?"

I jumped. It was Ralston.

"I . . . did you hear it?" I stammered.

"Hear what?"

"Something—shrieked." I pointed to the shadows.

He went to the place I had indicated and crouched down. "Come here," he said, "I'll show you."

Reluctantly I crossed the short distance. I heard him strike a match and in the yellow-blue flare I saw a cat tearing at a dead rat. I closed my eyes and shuddered.

"You did not know we had puss on board?" Ralston asked.

"Why, yes." I had forgotten. Roxanne and I had seen the cat on several occasions, an enormous tom with orange stripes, but it had darted away each time we had approached it.

"He is a good ratter," said Mr. Ralston.

"There are rats on *The Secret Duchess?*"

"Certainly there are rats. Every ship has them. Surely you have heard the expression, 'rats will leave a sinking ship?' It's the truth, and sometimes, I believe, I would trust a rat's intelligence, his instinct, above a man's."

"Yes," I said. "Still . . ." I shuddered again, thinking of our cabin and how I might wake up some morning to find one of those horrid creatures had shared my bed, or Roxanne's.

"I forgot," he said, in an annoying, patronizing tone, "women are squeamish about such things."

"You enjoy my discomfiture," I said. "I daresay you are not overly fond of rats yourself."

"No, but I do not quiver."

"I am not quivering!" I retorted, although I was—with rage. "Because one woman was a disappointment to you does not make us all weak and . . . and foolish. At least we do not drown ourselves in self-pity."

There was a small silence. I could not see his face, but surmised he was a little taken aback. "You are quite right," he said at last.

I began to walk away.

"Mrs. Hayworth . . ."

I turned.

"Please accept my apology."

"Knowing what an effort it must be for you to offer one, I accept." I left him there, standing in the shadows, not looking back.

The presence of rats did not put a stop to my nightly walks. I continued them, if for no other reason than to show Jonathan Ralston I was not the timid female he supposed me to be. Nor was I deterred by the persistent rumor seeping up from the crew that Ah Ching's ghost still walked. As far as I was concerned that particular phantom had been permanently laid to rest.

However, two nights after the rat episode I discovered, in a rather terrifying way, that rumor and fact were one—Ah Ching's spirit was still with us. I had made the turn at the corner of the galley and was heading aft along the rail when, coming opposite one of the small boats lashed to the rigging, I heard a thumping sound. Looking up, I saw the canvas cover on the boat moving; first a bulge here, then another there. My first reaction was that the *Duchess* was carrying, unknown to us, a stowaway, for their habitual hiding places, so I had read, were in the small boats. They would remain well concealed during the day, and at night, under cover of darkness, sneak out to forage for food.

There was a lantern above and to the side of the boat, and it gave a fair light, so what I saw was plain enough and not an illusion.

I stood for a moment debating whether to call one of the men or wait and see if anyone did emerge from the boat. The possibility occurred to me that my stowaway might turn out to be the ship's cat on his nocturnal rat hunt.

As I watched, the corner of the canvas slowly lifted, and what I saw drove all thoughts of stowaways and cats from my head.

A yellow hand had appeared, gripping the edge of the boat. Bright yellow with thick spatulate fingers. Before my riveted gaze it started to move cautiously, as if blindly feeling its way, carefully creeping down the side of the boat. No arm, no body, just that ugly yellow glove, a travesty of a hand. It paused as if aware of my terror-stricken presence, then the fingers humped themselves, mincing first to the right, then to the left, a sightless, glutted thing in a macabre jig.

It traveled upward again, halting at the rim, curling and slipping and clinging, turning palm upward. One finger began to beckon.

I ran then, ran in horror, stumbling over ropes and hatches and gear, not knowing where I was going, mindless, not caring, only wanting to get away from that creeping horror.

A voice called, but I ran on. "Mrs. Hayworth!" A hand on my arm brought me to an abrupt halt. "Mrs. Hayworth!" It was Mr. Hammersmith. "What has happened?"

"The boat . . ." I stammered. There were several of the crew behind him, peering curiously at me with white rimmed eyes.

"I . . . I saw something in . . . in the small boat . . ." I was on the verge of describing the yellow hand when I suddenly realized how intent the men were on my words, as if waiting, as they had done once before, for my confirmation of the rumored phantom.

"I . . . I think someone is hiding in the life boat." I pointed to it.

"Will one of you men take a look?" Mr. Hammersmith inquired.

No one moved.

"All right," he said, "I shall go myself."

He climbed up the rail and pulled back the canvas. "There is nothing here, Mrs. Hayworth," he said. "If you could come up, I would show you."

"No . . . no, I believe you."

At this point Adam arrived. "What seems to be the trouble?" he asked in a cold voice.

Mr. Hammersmith jumped down from the boat while I, in bumbling apology, said I hadn't meant to cause a disturbance. I did not dare tell Adam about the yellow hand. He had heard from Ralston my previous account and afterwards had accused me of having "mad fancies." "I thought there might be a stowaway," I explained rather unconvincingly.

Adam looked at me for a long moment. He was displeased, I could tell. "All right," he said. Then turning to the men, he barked, "What are you all gaping at? Taylor, get up there and see that the canvas is tightly secured."

It was not until later, when I had crawled between the sheets and laid my head on the pillow, that I wondered what Mr. Hammersmith was doing on the deck alone. I had never seen him there without Edith and, unlike me, he was not given to strolling at night. There was another nagging worry, something which I could not name or bring to mind. I tossed and turned for another hour going through the night's events. What was it that bothered me?

I was sinking down into the first layer of sleep, and it came to me with a jolt, dragging me back to wakefulness. Mr. Hammersmith, I remembered, had climbed up to the boat and lifted the canvas easily. As little as I understood of ships, I knew for a fact that the canvas on those small boats was fixed tightly, intricately, having watched the men undo just such a canvas when Billy had gone overboard. Had someone been in that boat, after all, not a ghost but someone very much alive?

I ought to tell Adam. If someone were hiding in boats and dark corners, pouncing out on the unwary, scaring them half to death, then Adam should know. But supposing the boat canvas had been loose because of a seaman's negligence? And supposing the yellow glove *was* the embodiment of Ah Ching's unhappy spirit, the thick false hand, the beckoning finger, a troubled spectre trying to convey a message to the living?

So I came full circle back to my original thought, my fear. The hand was something I did not understand; absurd, frightening—it existed. And I knew I could never speak of it to Adam.

As it was he was much upset with me. "If you are going to stir up a commotion at every shadow," he told me the next morning, "then I advise you to confine your walking to daytime hours."

Everything, after that night, slid steadily downhill. One of the hands, Woodley, I think was his name, died the first of the week. He was much older than most of the crew and had been ailing for some time, complaining of stomach pains. The cook had given him a cup of tea laced with rum the night before he died because he had said the pain was so bad. In the morning he was found dead in his bunk.

Burial, always prompt, if not hasty, at sea, was at two in the afternoon. It was a clear, beautiful day, the sea with a slight swell, the strong breeze fluttering the lowered ensign. Mr. Hammersmith gave the funeral oration, a rather lengthy one under the circumstances since he had never known the man, and had, in fact, to be corrected twice as to the deceased's name. I could well imagine how Mr. Hammersmith relished his present role. The services which he conducted each Sunday morning were ill attended and now he had the entire ship's complement plus all the passengers as his captive audience.

At last he had finished. The ship was hove to, the moan of the wind in the rigging stilled. The corpse was carried to the rail, the hatch on which it lay was tilted, and the shrouded figure slid into the sea with a dull plop. Looking down into the crystal, green-blue water I watched the weighted figure sink, sink. And then I saw a shadow darting over it, followed by another and another. There was a thrashing, a turmoil, the appearance of one lone, stark fin. Sharks!

I turned away depressed and sick. I did not think it a proper way for anyone's life to end, being thrown into the sea to make a feast for blood hungry predators.

Towards five o'clock Mr. Phipps came to Adam in the chartroom. My door was on the hook, so I not only saw him go in, but heard a good deal of the conversation. The men, Mr. Phipps told Adam, wanted Sam Ching to throw his father's ashes into the sea. "What was good enough for Woodley is good enough for the Chinaman."

"I cannot ask Mr. Ching to do anything of the sort," Adam replied.

"The hands is gettin' ugly," Mr. Phipps said. "They say the dead Chinaman is worse than a witch's hex. And some refuse to budge from the fo'castle unless the trunk goes over the rail."

"You realize, Mr. Phipps," said Adam in a voice which would have chilled stone, "that this is mutinous talk."

"Yes, sir, but . . ."

"And you are well aware, no doubt, of the punishment for mutiny?"

"It ain't me, sir, that's doing the talk. I was only reportin' . . ."

"I can well assure you that such punishment will be far more drastic and more painful than any imagined hex."

"Yes, sir, but . . ."

"There are no buts. Relay my words. Anyone who refuses to obey orders will be put 'tween decks to keep Mr. Griggs company. Is that plain?"

"Yes, sir."

I hastily shut my door, and a moment later I heard the bosun walk past.

I thought it quite admirable of Adam to defend Sam Ching in the face of a rebellious crew, risking mutiny for a handful of ashes. But then, of course, I did not know the whole story.

No sooner had the bosun gone down than Bella Kincaid came bursting from her cabin shouting she had been robbed. It brought us all out into the alleyway, including Adam. For some minutes Bella was so wildly incoherent no one could understand what had been stolen. Finally Adam managed to calm her down. "My pearl necklace," she breathed. "My *real* pearls. They're gone."

"Are you certain you haven't mislaid them?" Adam asked.

"Of course, I'm certain. I saw the pearls before I went to the funeral. They were right there in a little velvet box on top of the dressing table. A count gave that necklace to me. No one *but* a count would give a lady real pearls. Besides being very valuable, they're a sentimental treasure. My greatest treasure. And they're gone—gone! Some thief, some damned thief . . . !"

"Now, now," said Adam soothingly, before she could work herself into another lather. "Suppose Mrs. Hayworth helps you look through your cabin once more."

"Are you calling me a liar?" she demanded, hands on hips.

"Not at all," said Adam. "But I do not think it would do any harm to look, do you?"

"And give the thief time to get away?" Bella's bosom heaved.

"Where would he go?" Adam asked reasonably. "It is more than a thousand-mile swim to shore."

She looked at him. He smiled, and she capitulated. "All right then. If you promise . . ."

"I promise to question every last person on this ship. One way or the other you will find your pearls. I assure you of that, Mrs. Kincaid."

Bella's cabin was even more littered than when I had first seen it. She showed me the empty red velvet jeweler's box. "You see," she said, "you see."

"When did you last wear the necklace?" I asked.

"At dinner. Yesterday." Her face was still mottled with anger.

"Perhaps you put it somewhere else?" I said, looking around.

"No, I'm very careful about the pearls. A count gave them to me."

"I hope you don't mind my looking . . ."

"Go ahead, help yourself." She sat heavily down on the bunk and, reaching to the floor, brought up a gin bottle. She poured herself a drink. "Look away."

I started with the dressing table, shaking out a pair of

stockings, a yellow, frayed corset, several soiled handkerchiefs, carefully folding and putting them on a chair. It was not a pleasant task, this literal going through of Bella's dirty linen, but I hadn't any choice. If it turned out, as I began to fear, that the pearls had been stolen then Adam, again, would have a troublesome mystery on his hands. I had reached the bottom of the heap when I was brought up short by the sight of a pair of gloves. They were long, elbow-length ball gloves. And they were a bright yellow. I stared at them, my mind going back to the gloved hand which had crept so insidiously, horribly down the side of the small boat. But that, I reminded myself, had been a short glove with thick fingers, not like this one at all. Yet if the fingers were stuffed with paper, the top tucked inward . . .

"Did you find them?" Bella asked.

"No. These gloves, Bella," I said, turning with the gloves in my hand. "They are very elegant. I have never seen you wear them."

"Here?" she asked in scorn. "After I got all gussied up that first night, I wouldn't bother again."

"I suppose you have a point there." I slipped one of the gloves on.

"Say," she said, "why . . ." And she began to laugh, that raucous loud laugh of hers which never failed to bring a smile to my lips.

"What is so funny?" I wanted to know.

"The gloves," she said. "I bet five dollars you think I've been parading around as the Chinaman's ghost."

I colored and quickly removed the glove. "C'mon, that's what you're thinking, isn't it?"

"It passed through my mind," I said.

She laughed again. "Well, if that ain't the funniest thing I've heard yet. Now why would I want to do a dumb thing like that?"

I shrugged. "I guess it was silly."

"Silly? It's downright crazy. I admit I'm bored out of my skull. But playing half-wit jokes ain't my idea of fun. Now if I had a man friend to entertain, say someone like that Mr. Ralston . . ."

"Mr. Ralston is a woman-hater," I said crossly, suddenly annoyed at the sight of her swigging gin.

"Them's the best kind," she assured me knowingly. "Once you get . . ."

"I do not want to talk about Mr. Ralston!" I shot at her.

She looked at me with raised eyebrows and I turned away,

a little surprised at my own vehemence. "It . . . it is just that I do not care to gossip," I explained. But was that it? Or was it because I did not want to think of Bella, an experienced woman of the world, throwing out a net for Mr. Ralston? Jealous? But that was preposterous!

I began to go through the drawers, hastily, thoroughly, hating the chore Adam had assigned me more than ever. Next I went to the cupboards, opening each with a bang of the doors. They were bare except for a round hat box, two long dresses, one shoe. I shut them and strode to the washstand.

The pearls were there in a half mug of stale gin. The clasp had turned green. "Here!" I said triumphantly, resisting the urge to throw them at her.

"Well, I'll be damned," she said, lumbering to her feet. "You sweet thing." She took them and gave me a heavy, gin soaked hug. "I'm ever so grateful . . ." Large tears came to her eyes.

"I think it would be a good idea to put them in the ship's safe. Adam has one in the chartroom."

"I'd rather have them with me." She looped the necklace about her neck, fumbling for a minute with the clasp. "I'll sleep with them. I'll never take them off. And thank you, again, my dear."

"You are welcome," I said, going to the door.

"Charlotte, wait!"

I turned.

"I made a scene again, didn't I?"

"It is over," I said. "It does not matter."

"It . . . I don't want you to have a bad opinion of me."

I wondered why my opinion should matter to her. "You could not help what you felt."

"Listen . . . you've got to understand. The pearls are all I have left in the world."

"I am sorry."

"You see," she went on, "it's true I made a lot of money in my time. A lot of money. But it went, and then at the end there was the girls to pay off, and the laundress, the cook, and the grocer. And the lawyers. Venal men. So I was left with nothing but the fare to Melbourne—and these." She fingered the pearls. "They're my stake to start a new life. Do you understand?"

I nodded.

"No, you don't. You've never been poor."

I saw no point in telling her that I had had my share of

penny pinching, and once, unbelievable as it seemed now, had come close to the poorhouse.

Tears glistened in Bella's eyes again. "It's not being a pauper so much as being alone. I have no family, no husband. I ran away from home when I was twelve. I won't tell you the story of my life, how I was seduced into selling myself. The tale is too long. But now here I am, not young anymore, all on my own with no one to fend for me. And that's why the pearls mean so much." She sat down on the bunk and dabbed at her eyes with a handkerchief.

"I am glad I found them, then," I said, softened, regretting my former anger.

But later when I talked about it to Mathilda, she turned down her mouth. "I wouldn't waste too much sympathy on that one. From what I've seen of madams, they're a hardheaded lot. I doubt Bella is an exception. Anyone who would earn their livelihood battening on the misery of others—and those girls are miserable—can't afford to be sentimental. They'd steal their grandmother's eyes if they saw profit in it."

Adam was not surprised when I told him I had found Bella Kincaid's pearls. In fact, he hardly seemed to hear what I had to say. "Yes," he remarked absently, as he sat in a chair, smoking his cigar. "I thought as much."

"She apologized for having made a scene," I added.

He did not say anything, but sat watching the spiral of smoke from his cigar.

"Adam," I said, going to him on impulse and kneeling at his feet. "Are you sorry I came?"

He looked at me, his eyes coming back from some long distance. "No, of course not. What an odd thing to say."

"Sometimes I wonder. I know you are having a difficult time . . ."

"I did not expect it to be easy." He gave me a weak smile.

I wanted more than that. I wanted him to kiss me, to hold me, to tell me that I was his love, his life, that he was happy, happy to have me by his side. I put my head on his knee to hide the tears that suddenly burned behind my eyes. He patted my head as he would the ship's cat.

"Charlotte," he said, "were you in the chartroom today?"

"Why no," I said, raising my face in surprise. "What makes you ask that?"

"Someone was there. Not Mr. Ralston, someone who should not have been."

"Was anything taken?"

"No. Maps had been moved, a sextant. But nothing taken."

"Was the chartroom locked?"

"I have not kept it locked. Now, of course, I shall have to."

"Someone was searching through it then? But for what?"

He hesitated a moment. "I can make a good guess. It was a key. The key to Sam Ching's cabin."

"But Adam, it is missing. I neglected to tell you. The night Mr. Hammersmith was worried about Ching, I . . ."

"The key is not missing," he broke in. "I have it. And whoever wants it shall jolly well have to deal with me first."

CHAPTER EIGHT

Adam's statement uttered with such grim stubbornness upset me. Otherwise I don't think I would have told him I knew the crew was on the verge of mutiny and that I guessed it was one among them, frightened by Ah Ching's ghost, who had been in the chartroom searching for the key.

The look on his face was enough to tell me I had made a mistake by speaking out. "And how did you know about the crew?" he asked in a tight, controlled voice.

"I could not help overhearing Mr. Phipps . . ."

"And so you listened at the keyhole like a common servant?"

That set me off. "You would risk the whole ship for the sake of an old man's ashes." I was so angry I forgot to lower my voice. "Or is it mulish pride?"

"*The Duchess is* my pride. I made a promise that she would carry Ah Ching to his final resting place and that she will do."

"*She!*" I uttered in disgust.

One word led to another and we had a terrible quarrel, the worst yet. After Adam had finally stormed out of the cabin and I was left to nurse my wounds, I was sorry. But the damage had been done, hateful words spoken to each other, words which could never be taken back. I tried not to blame the *Duchess* for driving us apart. But it was impossible not to. *She*, he had called her, *my pride*. Once more I thought of the ship as Adam's paramour, my rival. Worse. A real woman I could face, could fight. But not this winged, hulled creature with dark alleyways, her haunted decks, her intimate knowledge of Adam's beloved sea.

Then I began to think that maybe it was not the ship. Perhaps I was placing my blame and hatred on something which ill deserved it. Sam Ching had been the bone of our contention, Sam Ching whose face we never saw, who hid behind a locked door, guarding his father's precious ashes. I could almost sympathize with the crew, share in their superstition, their fear and dislike. If the little man had never come aboard, if the urn could be tossed into the sea, if . . .

I brought myself up abruptly. Such thoughts were wrong, disloyal. I must put them behind me. I was Adam's wife, Mrs. "Captain" Hayworth. I must stick by him, abide by his decisions no matter how much pain it caused me.

And the pain was there like a thorn in my side. Oh, how I longed for the sight of land, for a rock rising out of the sea, a bit of island, anything to show we were nearing journey's end. But I knew there would be nothing until we reached Shanghai. Shanghai. I carried the name like a talisman close to my heart, a promise, a turning point, an end to our troubles.

My distress was augmented by the shameful suspicion that the others were aware, had most probably heard Adam and me quarreling. That suspicion became a certainty when I saw Mathilda late that afternoon. She was too tactful, of course, to allude to the matter directly, but instead she spoke of her own marriage, how she and Roddy had fought, sometimes comically, sometimes vigorously over the years—thirty it was now—and were the better for it, more fond of one another than ever. "There's nothing like a good honest spat to clear the air," she said. I wanted to tell her that our "spat" had done nothing of the sort.

What mortified me most of all was that Ralston should know. Even if he had not heard the sharp words between Adam and me, he could not help but notice the coolness, the formality with which we addressed one another. And I could imagine his thinking, "I was right. Ships and wives don't mix."

It seemed to me there was nothing more shameful, more degrading than the exposure of a marriage gone bad. If we had been still living in London, or in our own small house on Beacon Street, fighting and raving at one another, only a servant or two would have been the wiser. But here on the ship, a small confined world, where any small item of interest was pounced on, vulturelike, and picked clean, our quarreling would offer a fresh and tasty morsel of gossip. I would have gladly remained in the cabin, like Sam Ching, incognito, until we reached Shanghai. But in so doing I knew I would only add to speculation. I envisioned Bella, especially, leaning forward across the table and saying in a hushed, confidential tone, "I believe the captain is having trouble with his wife. My guess is she's taken a fancy to his first mate, a handsome man, and he's had to lock her up. Of course, I don't blame *her* . . ." So pride, no matter how foolish, dictated my continued appearance on deck and in the saloon.

Dinner proved to be the most unpleasant part of the day. Not daring to leave Roxanne alone in the cabin since our trouble with Griggs, I would bring her to the saloon sleepy and often out of sorts. Sometimes Adam would be there, sometimes Mr. Ralston, depending on who had the watch. Neither of them spoke much, Adam having given up the pretense of genial host. Both men, whichever presided at the table, would eat hurriedly, leaving before dessert. A long tenuous silence would often follow. Edith would sit staring into her plate, Mr. Hammersmith and Bella busy with their food, but nonetheless managing between forkfuls to cast little sly glances my way. Then, invariably, Thomas Hammersmith would commence a sermon on the blessings of connubial harmony. Thankfully, I was saved from too much of this by Mathilda, who with a smile would turn the conversation.

It was not difficult to do so, for next to sermonizing Thomas Hammersmith liked to talk about himself. During those long, interminable meals we got the full story of his past, from the time he left home at fifteen with only five dollars in his pocket and a Bible until a Reverend Bleaker, impressed by his preaching, asked him to do missionary work in Canton.

"They are paying you no salary?" Mathilda asked him once.

"None, but our passage and a small sum to get us started. It is a pity because, as I have said, we have such beautiful plans. But the Lord will provide, of that I am sure."

It was on a Saturday, I remember, we ran into another calm, our third, one that lasted close to a week. On the afternoon of the second day, the engines stopped. We had run out of coal and we could do nothing but sit in the midst of that endless sea, quiet and placid, gently rocking and creaking, helpless to move. A grim-faced Adam had a chair brought up to the poop and there he took all his meals, eating and sleeping at his post.

On the afternoon of the fourth day we sighted a steamship on the horizon. The men quickly ran up signals, hoping to get some fuel from her, but apparently she did not see our flags drooping in the calm and steamed steadily on, a smoking smudge disappearing slowly from view.

Bella was the first to notice that our meals had become skimpy. She was certain we were down to our last breadcrust and saw herself reduced to gnawing on the rigging, quenching her thirst with a ration of one teaspoon of water a day. Mr. Ralston assured her that we would have plenty if we all ate a little less, and certainly, he added pointedly, it would do no harm to our figures.

Five days had gone by, and still no wind. I was sitting on the deck with Roxanne on my lap reading to her when I became aware of Mr. Ralston standing beside us listening.

"You enjoy *Grimm's Fairy Tales?*" I asked with a smile.

"I did when I was no bigger than Roxanne here," he replied.

His answer surprised me because I could not picture Mr. Ralston, no matter how I tried, as a youngster, or ever having been captivated by anything as childish as a fairy tale.

"You are welcome to sit and listen, if you like," I invited.

Roxanne chimed in. "Oh yes, do." Inexplicably, the way children do, she had taken a liking to Mr. Ralston. He in turn, again to my surprise, while never demonstrative, seemed to have a fondness for her, too.

"No, thank you," Mr. Ralston said. "I would not want anyone to think I had gone daft as Mr. Griggs, suddenly beguiled by the brothers Grimm."

"How is the poor man?" I inquired.

He shook his head. "Not good. He refuses to eat now. He is willing himself to death."

"He feels he has nothing to live for, I suppose."

"I have no patience with men like Griggs. Weak is what they are."

"And you have never been such?" I asked pointedly.

"Never." His mouth clamped on the word, less like a man who was once intrigued by fairy tales than ever.

"Do you think the wind will come up soon?" I asked after a pause.

"I do not know. This calm is strange, very strange. We should not have it at all in this latitude." He looked out toward the horizon and I followed his gaze. In the distance between sky and sea I saw an odd white line.

"Look," I said, "a cloud bank. Doesn't that usually portend a good wind?"

Mr. Ralston said nothing but continued to stare, a small furrow growing deeper between his eyes. "Those are not clouds . . . they . . . oh, my God!"

He snatched Roxanne from me, at the same time pulling me roughly to my feet. "The alleyway . . ."

I looked over his shoulder and saw with stunned horror that what I had supposed was a cloud bank was a gigantic wave, a mighty upheaval of the ocean unlike any of the white capped seas which had buffeted us during the storm. There was a shout, "For God's sake, hold on. It's got us." Ralston's arm tightened around me, his other hand grasping a stanchion.

I watched, horror stricken, a moment, no more than two drawn out into an eternity of suspense, and then it hit us with a shattering impact, a white surge of foam. I felt the ship lifted and flung forward like a bit of flotsam in the breaking surf. Gasping and struggling for breath under tons of water, I went through all the sensations of drowning, my mouth opened in a soundless scream, my hands clawing at Ralston. The end, my panic driven mind clamored, the end. That it should come to this, after all our hopes, our dreams. And Roxanne . . .

Then it was over. I could hardly believe it. I was alive and Roxanne, too, both of us still clinging to Mr. Ralston.

"Start pumping!" he shouted over my shoulder. Then to me, "Are you all right?"

I must have been a sight with the water streaming through my hair, my gown plastered to my body, but I was so grateful to be there, the ship still under us, I hardly gave it a thought.

"Thank you, Mr. Ralston," I said, impulsively planting a kiss on his cheek.

His face turned dark, dark as a thundercloud. "Do not . . . do not ever do that again." Then stopping a passing sailor he said, "Here, help Mrs. Hayworth and the child to her cabin."

Everything in the ship was awash. The water had come into all the cabins and I spent the rest of the afternoon and evening wringing out blankets and clothes. Adam, looking in to see how we were, explained that we had been in the path of a tidal wave which probably had its origin in an oceanic upheaval many thousands of miles away.

By some miracle no one was lost overboard, no one was hurt. But it shook us all. The crew grumbled and muttered among themselves as they sullenly went about the task of clearing the deck of tangled gear. Bella twittered and fidgeted as if she had come down with St. Vitus Dance, complaining she had run out of gin and that Cookie would not give her an extra bottle of wine to tide her over. Mr. Hammersmith took to hymn singing, and Edith seemed to have shrunk to a shadow with two enormous eyes. Only Mathilda was unperturbed, knitting away with a steady clack-clack, serene and confident.

That evening the wind freshened, and we sailed on. San Francisco, the busy wharf, the peopled houses clinging to the hills behind it had become a dim memory. Trees and earth and cobblestoned streets belonged to a past I could scarcely remember. The sea was endless, vast, an immense loneliness surrounding us. What next, I thought wearily. What could possibly happen next?

It was another fire.

The first I knew of it was when Roxanne, tugging at my arm in the dead of night, awakened me. "Mama," she said in a small voice. "I smell something funny."

I sat up sniffing. There was an odor similar to the smoking of a paraffin lamp. A glance at our own lamps showed them to be clean. I got out of bed, my nostrils flared and quivering. The smell was coming from the alleyway. I opened the door and saw a small crackling flame opposite Sam Ching's door.

I ducked back and, snatching the blanket from my bed, rushed out and threw it over the fire. Then, to make sure I had smothered it thoroughly, I got Roxanne's blanket too and a pitcher of water. The flame sizzled and sputtered, then died.

Mathilda opened her door, struggling into her camel's hair dressing gown, her hair tousled. "What is it, Charlotte?"

I put my finger to my lips. I did not want to wake the others. "A fire," I whispered.

"What? Not again?"

"Again," I said. "And this time I do not think it was Mr. Griggs."

"Someone in the crew?"

"I am sure of it. Would you do something for me?"

"Yes, anything, of course."

"Stay with Roxanne. I am going to get Adam."

He was dozing in his chair, his head hung sideways. When I touched his arm, he started, his eyes flying open, his face paling in the overhanging light. "What are you doing here?" he asked.

I told him about the fire and he sprang to his feet. "You put it out?" he asked.

"Yes, but I thought . . ."

"Does anyone else know?"

"Only Mathilda Jackson."

"Good." He helped me down the ladder.

"It seems to me someone is trying to smoke Sam Ching out of his cabin," I said. "Even if they have to burn the ship. Is the feeling against him that strong?"

He did not answer.

"If I were you . . ."

"Charlotte," he said angrily. "Please don't badger me."

There he was again, slamming the door in my face. For a moment I was tempted to tell him I did not care if the *Duchess* frizzled to the water line, but then we were in the alleyway and I was helping him fold the charred blankets.

I thanked Mathilda, and we said our good nights without further comment as Adam stowed the burnt blankets in the drawers beneath the bunk. He went and got fresh blankets from a storeroom at the end of the passage. I tucked Roxanne snugly back into her bed, and Adam came in and kissed her, holding her for a long moment against his shoulder. There was no such loving comfort for me.

"Adam, please stay," I said. "I am frightened."

"There is no need to be."

"How can you say that?"

"Because I will take care of things. Don't you trust me?"

"Yes . . . but . . ."

"Pull yourself together, Charlotte. Once we reach Shanghai our troubles will be over." And then, as an afterthought, he bent and kissed me coldly on the cheek.

Once we reached Shanghai. How absurd, I thought. We will never get there. And even if we do, how many troubles in between?

Two nights later my question was answered in a most horrible manner.

It had been a dull, cloudy day, unusually hot and sultry. I retired early, snuffing out the lamp, lying down in the dark, wide eyed and tense. The cabin seemed to have shrunk around me even more, the walls pressing on my fevered brain. I tossed and turned, pummeling the pillows, rearranging them, finally shoving them on to the floor. "Pull yourself together," that was what Adam had said. It was all very well for *him* to say, I thought bitterly, occupied with physical tasks, with the need to make decisions, to chart, to pilot, to sail the ship. But for me time was heavy, and I had nothing to do but think, think.

I was still awake when I heard the splatter of rain against the porthole. Ah, I thought, relief. If I could only feel a few drops on my hot face. One breath of cool air. I got up and pulled on my dressing gown. I would only go to the head of the alleyway.

I closed the door softly and made my way down the dim passage. When I got opposite Sam Ching's door I noticed it was open a crack. Perhaps the poor man was seeking air too.

Curious and feeling rather childish, I put my eye to the crack. What I saw will haunt my dreams forever.

A lamp had been placed on the floor and it cast its yellow light upward on a tall figure in black oilskins poised above the bunk. Even in the uncertain light I could see the knife. It went down with a sudden plunge. There was a stifled gurgle and the knife went down and up and down again.

I must have unconsciously pushed the door wider, for it suddenly swung inward. The figure straightened. I could not see the face, a sou'wester was pulled low over it. For a long, eternal, suspended moment the faceless figure and I stared at one another. And then full horror descended upon me and I turned, a strangled, frozen scream rising in my breast. I stumbled on the hem of my gown, my hands groping wildly when a sudden sharp pain struck the back of my head. A thousand splintered sparks danced before my eyes.

And then there was nothing.

CHAPTER NINE

When I opened my eyes I was lying on my bunk, and for a few moments I wondered why I had gone to bed still wearing my dressing gown and slippers and why my head hurt so. I tried to sit up and pain, like a tight, stabbing cap, jarred my teeth.

I remembered everything then; going out for a breath of air, Sam Ching's open door, the figure in oilskins. And the knife. Someone had plunged it into Sam Ching. He was hurt, perhaps dead.

How I had reached my cabin, my bed, was something, oddly enough, I did not ponder. My only thought was to get help and quickly.

With a hand pressed to my head to contain the pain I began to ease myself out of bed just as Adam came through the door.

His face was white, his eyes like thunder. "What are you doing?" he asked. "Here, lie back and don't move." He was wearing oilskins and they glistened with rain. "I've brought you some brandy."

"Adam, I saw something terrible happen."

"Here," he said, pouring the brandy into a small tumbler, "you had best drink and then I will have another look at your bump."

"Adam . . . I am . . . I don't *want* the brandy," I stammered in exasperation. "I am trying to tell you that someone, someone stabbed Sam Ching with a knife. Don't you understand?"

He did not answer, but bent over me, his fingers probing under my hair.

"You do not seem one bit concerned," I said.

"I *am* concerned, damn it," he said in sudden anger. "How in heaven's name did you get to Sam Ching's doorstep?"

"I was going out for a breath of air, his door was partly open . . ."

"Why don't you stay in your cabin where you belong at

night? Why in God's name do you have to go prowling about?"

"I was not prowling. I told you I went out for some air. Am I supposed to be a prisoner?"

"It is not a bad idea. Here . . ." He held out the tumbler.

"*I do not want the brandy!* Why are you not listening to me?"

"I am listening. I know about Sam Ching. Who do you think found you unconscious?"

"You saw then . . . ?"

"I saw you on his doorstep crumpled in a heap."

"And Sam Ching?"

"He is dead."

"Oh, my God. Who . . . ?"

He sat down beside me and took hold of my shoulder, his fingers digging into my flesh. "I thought you could tell me."

I shook my head.

"How much did you see?"

"I . . . someone in oilskins and a hat with a knife."

"You did not see the face?"

"No . . . no . . ."

"Can you give me any sort of description?"

I closed my eyes and in my mind I saw the figure in the yellow lamplight, his shadow cast grotesquely on the wall. "He was tall . . . he didn't make a sound. That is all I can tell you."

He got up and put the brandy bottle on the table.

"Adam . . . how did whoever it was manage to get into Ching's cabin in the first place?"

"By impersonating Cookie. You are not the only one to-night with a lump on your head. It seems Cookie was in the habit of visiting Sam Ching late each night sharing a cup of tea, a pipe. Someone waylaid him, struck him, and took his oilskins."

"And he did not see or recognize who it was?"

"No."

"But why . . . why should Sam Ching be *killed*? For an urn of ashes? I should think just threatening him would be enough."

Adam picked up the tumbler, stared at it a minute, and then drank it down. "He was not killed for those ashes," he said.

"Why . . . why then?"

He did not look at me. "I cannot tell you."

The blood rushed to my face, causing my head to throb

anew. "You cannot tell me," I said in derision. "What is it you tell me anymore? Nothing. I am excess baggage on this ship. Ballast—a bag of sand. Something which could have very well been left behind on the wharf when you sailed and never missed."

Still he kept his eyes averted.

"Adam . . . Adam, what has happened between us? Has our love gone, died, everything we have been through together, does it mean nothing to you?"

"That is not true. You must be patient," he said.

"I have been patient. You asked me to trust you. Can you not do the same for me?"

"It is for your own safety."

"Oh," I said. "Ching had gold, then. Bella was right."

Adam sighed, a long, heavy sigh. "It was not gold, but something . . ." He stopped and turned to me, his eyes boring into mine. "Promise, Charlotte, on your word of honor, you will tell no one. No one."

"Why should you find it necessary to ask me to swear to it? Of course, I promise."

He hesitated a few moments, then began to speak. "Ching had with him another object, one that was of inestimable value. A statue of a Buddha. About a foot high, it was of solid gold, encrusted with precious gems: diamonds, rubies, emeralds . . ."

"*Was*, you say."

"It was stolen tonight, Charlotte."

"How did Ching come by it?"

"It is a long, rather complicated and bloody story from what I could gather. Originally it was filched from the temple by a monk who was later robbed of it by a rice merchant and so on. Eventually, how was never made clear to me, it came into the hands of a coolie who brought it to the United States when he was contracted to work on the railroad. This coolie had befriended Sam Ching's father in a place called Rainbow Creek . . ."

"Rainbow Creek!" I exclaimed. "Bella has been there and both the Hammersmiths . . ."

"I suppose many people know the place. In years past it was rather a large mining center. At any rate the coolie took sick, knew he was dying and gave the Buddha to Ah Ching, making him promise he would return it to China. Ah Ching could not go at once. He had a large family and lacked the means for such a long journey. However, in due course, he managed to scrape enough gold from the played out mines around Rainbow Creek to enable him to open a shop in San Francisco. There he prospered. He was preparing to make the journey when he was killed."

"For the Buddha?"

"Possibly. Mr. Ching thought so. Knowing his father's desire to return the Buddha to its proper place and also to be buried one day in his native Canton, Sam, the eldest son, undertook the journey."

"And you knew all this when you allowed Ching to book passage?" I asked.

"No, I did not. If I had, perhaps I would have refused him."

"Then how did you find out?"

"I went to Mr. Ching shortly after we left San Francisco. The men were already beginning to complain about the ashes and bad luck. I did not want trouble. I thought perhaps I could persuade Ching to have the ashes buried at sea. But no, he refused. I said I would not force him then. I understood. It was when I was ready to leave he stopped me.

" 'You are a trustworthy person,' he said. 'One with much heart. There is something I must ask of you. If it so happens I do not survive the voyage, will you take the contents of the trunk and myself to our destination?'

" 'Your father is one thing,' I told him. 'But as for you, it would be impossible. We must bury our dead at sea.'

"He thought for a moment. 'Very well. But this trunk . . . I would not tell you, but I have a strange premonition. There is more than an urn with my honored father's remains here.' And then he told me about the Buddha. I was not happy about it, not happy at all. I asked Ching, 'Does anyone else know of this?' He answered, 'Mr. Loo, the cook. He is a cousin. I was not going to tell him, but he had already guessed.'

" 'Cookie is a gossip,' I said to Ching. 'He has already passed the word along that your father was murdered.'

" 'He is a foolish man,' Ching said. 'But not a malicious gossip. I do not think he realized how the crew would feel about Ah's violent death. Concerning the Buddha, however, he has sworn not to say a word. And you . . . you will tell no one, please?'

" 'I must inform Mr. Ralston. He is my second in command.'

" 'He is an honest man?'

" 'I trust him completely.'

Adam got up and poured himself another brandy. "I offered to take the statue and put it in the ship's safe, but Ching would not hear of it. He said he would remain in his cabin and protect the valuable image himself. I advised him to admit no one, to keep his door locked, and as an extra precaution to bolt it from the inside. But it seems to have done little good."

"Oh, Adam," I said. "It is so awful. You have no idea who did it?"

"None."

"You will have the *Duchess* searched?"

"Ralston and I will do it quietly. Can you imagine what a set-to it would cause were it known a valuable object such as the Buddha was stolen? Why, the hands would rip the ship apart searching for it. And as for Ching—I have no intention of making it known the way in which he died."

"The murder was a horrible thing—terrible," I said. "And I can see how you might blame yourself. But surely the Buddha is not your responsibility?"

"Everything on the *Duchess* is my responsibility. Including you."

"Well, I shall be all right. I have a thick skull." I gave him a wry smile.

"Charlotte, how thick *is* that skull?" he said, annoyed. "Don't you realize the situation you have placed yourself in?"

I gave him a blank look.

"You saw a murder done."

"But . . . but I told you. I did not see the face. It was too dark."

"The murderer does not know that." He paused, letting his words sink in.

They did. Sank and congealed into a lump of ice in the pit of my stomach. "You mean . . . ?"

"Your life might very well be in danger. Then, too, Charlotte, there is always the possibility the blow you received obliterated the memory of that face. One of these days you will remember . . ."

"No . . . no, I tell you I did not see it."

"I wish to God I could be with you. But I cannot. There's the ship . . ."

"Yes, the ship." I tried not to make my voice sound bitter. But Adam had a fine ear.

"The ship," he said acidly, "is our bread and butter." He got up and went to the door, his face in shadow. "I beg you to remain in the cabin until we get to Shanghai."

"How can I? There is Roxanne. I cannot keep her caged in . . . in this place. And the others, they will want to know why I do not come to the dining saloon."

He thought for a moment. "I suppose you are right. Above all I want to keep this whole thing as hushed as possible. Especially your part in it." He came and stood beside me. "How brave are you?"

"I don't know," I answered slowly. "Not very."

"Then you will have to be—very. Say nothing of what has happened tonight. Nothing. Go about your daily routine as usual, except take care never to be alone with just one person."

"The passengers? Surely you do not think . . ."

"The passengers. Anybody. Everybody."

"Not even Mrs. Jackson?"

"Not even Mrs. Jackson."

"But, Adam, she is my friend. My *only* friend aboard ship. I haven't much to do with the others, and if I did not have her . . ."

"All right then," he said impatiently. "I suppose I am being overly suspicious. Mrs. Jackson, but no one else. In the morning we shall consign Sam Ching to the sea. And with him his father's ashes."

"The ashes?" I said, surprised at his abrupt change of mind. "You have been telling me all along you gave your word . . ."

"I do not care what I gave. A man has been murdered. The crew is close to mutiny as it is. I am sick unto death of their mutterings, their talk of ghosts. No more. I cannot risk it. The ashes go."

So we had another burial—Sam Ching's, his shrouded corpse sliding down to the waiting hungry sea. And with him went the urn containing his father's ashes.

If Adam had thought he could hide the cause of Ching's death, or that a valuable idol had been stolen, he was grossly mistaken. Cookie, having slept off his knock on the head, awoke in the afternoon and, upon being told of his countryman's demise, began to shout that Sam had been murdered. Mathilda and I heard him from the galley as we sat side by side on deck. "My knife!" he screamed in a voice that must have reached every nook and cranny of the *Duchess*. "It's gone. They killed him, they killed him for the Celestial Buddha!"

Mathilda turned to me. "Whatever can he mean by the Buddha?"

"I don't know," I said, hating myself for the lie.

Bella knew. That night at dinner when everyone had been

seated round the table, she leaned forward. "I had a feeling the Chinaman had something in that trunk besides ashes."

"Gold?" said Mr. Hammersmith.

"No. Didn't you hear Cookie this afternoon raving about a Buddha?"

"Why yes," said Mr. Hammersmith, "but I supposed he was calling upon his heathen god."

"No," she said. "It was the Celestial Buddha. An idol of solid gold, all stuck with jewels."

"Is that so?" said Mathilda, an amused half smile on her lips.

"That's so," said Bella. "When I had my boarding . . ." She caught herself, and none too soon. ". . . that is to say, when I had a season at Rainbow Creek and was staying at this boarding house, one of the roomers had a friend who told him about it. Said it belonged to some Chinaman. Now I am sure it was Ching."

"How can you be so certain?" I asked, making my voice casual, knowing there could not have been two such Buddhas, at least not in Rainbow Creek.

"Why else would Cookie be yelling 'he was killed for the Buddha?' "

Mr. Hammersmith cleared his throat. "Now that you mention it, I remember hearing a rumor of that sort. But then all kinds of rumors went around the camps, some of them quite preposterous. There was one . . ."

While he was speaking I noticed Roxanne nodding in her plate. I gathered her up and put her on the padded bench under the windows where she promptly curled into a ball and fell sound asleep. When I got back to the table Hammersmith was still talking. ". . . and as a result I do not give too much credence to rumors."

There was a small silence.

"The rumor is true," Edith spoke up.

We all looked at her. That she had broken her customary silence was surprising enough, but her announcement, to me at least, was as startling as if she had suddenly stood up and danced a jig. Was she going to reveal her sordid connection with Rainbow Creek after all?

"I saw it," she said, coloring under our collective stare.

Her husband put his hand out and covered hers. "My dear, surely . . ."

"Not in Rainbow Creek," she said hurriedly. "But in San Francisco. It was just after I married you, Thomas, and you said we were to go as missionaries to China. That it was our calling, remember?"

"Why, yes . . ."

"And I . . . *we* decided in order to prepare ourselves before we left we ought to go into Chinatown and work among the people there?"

"Yes, yes, I remember."

"Well, one afternoon I was on my rounds and I went into this little shop, and there was an elderly Chinese sitting there . . ."

"Ah Ching?" Bella asked.

"I don't know what his name was. They . . . the names sound all the same to me. He wore pantaloons and a cap, and he had the old-fashioned long queue, and on his left hand was a funny yellow glove . . ."

Ah Ching! It *had* been Ah Ching.

". . . I had my Bible and I started to explain, but I could tell, even though he listened politely, he didn't understand a word. Presently he got up and bowed and smiled, and I guessed he wanted me to leave. I was halfway down the street when it suddenly came to me, maybe that wasn't what he wanted at all. Maybe he thought for me to wait while he fetched someone to interpret. And I had gone! So I turned and hurried back. The shade in the window was down, but the door, though it caught a little, wasn't locked. I went in. The shop was empty, but there was a door behind a beaded curtain and, going to it, I peeped through. And there it was! Oh, I've never seen such a sight! The gold shining, the rubies, dark as blood and the green emeralds . . ." She stopped, her face turning scarlet.

"An idol," said Hammersmith in disgust. "A heathen idol. It ought to be melted down and used to pay for the feeding of the poor."

"It would feed quite a few," said Bella. "It is probably worth a fortune, a fortune." Her eyes had an avid luster.

It is like a fever, I thought. Because I, too, in my mind, pictured the golden Buddha quite clearly, the glitter, the iridescent jewels catching the candlelight, and how its priceless worth might buy and sell *The Secret Duchess* more than once over.

"Well," said Mathilda, cutting through the silence in a dry voice, "I, like Mr. Hammersmith, have heard many fantastic stories. But you know the old saying, 'seeing is believing.' It is all talk, idle talk. If the man was murdered it was because of the ashes, and nothing else. Mark my word, one of the crew did him in for that urn. That's the plain and simple fact of it."

But it was not plain, and it was not simple and far from fact. Ching had been killed. The Celestial Buddha not only existed, but it had been stolen. The murderer might have killed the Chinese for the ashes and, finding the Buddha, stolen it, leaving the urn behind, or he may not have. And unless the guilty party was found, we would never know.

Mr. Ralston had arrived at the tail end of our conversation. He had eaten in silence, seemingly impervious to the talk around him. I lingered after the others had gone, sipping at a cup of coffee I did not want, until the steward went through the door with a clattering tray of dishes and we were left alone.

"Mr. Ralston," I said. "They know."

"It is only supposition on their part." He leaned back, pushing his empty cup from him.

"But isn't that enough?"

"I suppose so. It is hard to keep any sort of secret for long aboard ship." He gave me a penetrating look. "That is why I think you would do well to follow your husband's advice."

"He told you?"

He nodded in the affirmative. "Go to your cabin, Mrs. Hayworth. He was right, you know. Trust no one."

"Surely," I said, smiling, "I can trust you. You are the last person I could ever imagine coveting a golden Buddha, or coveting anything for that matter."

"You are quite wrong, Mrs. Hayworth. I covet a good many things." His eyes burned into mine, and for a few heart-skipping moments it seemed I caught a glimpse of the man behind the stolid mask, a man of will, of determination, a man of passion. It was as if a chasm had suddenly opened at my feet, unknown until now and frightening.

Then the next moment the look was gone, and he was pushing back his chair, getting abruptly to his feet. "Good night," he said in a cold, formal voice.

Mathilda was waiting for me at the top of the stairs. "What ever did you say to Mr. Ralston?" she asked, taking the sleeping Roxanne from my arms. "He nearly knocked me over in his hurry. He was like a man running away from a fire."

"I cannot think what . . ."

"I wouldn't be at all surprised if that man was in love with you," she said smiling.

"Nonsense! He does not believe in love. He told me so, himself." But my words, even to my own ears, were far from convincing. "There are many things I covet," he had said. Another man's wife? No. I must not think of it. Ralston was honest, he was loyal, he could be trusted. Adam had told me so, and Adam knew Ralston well.

"I was only teasing," Mathilda laughed. "I know you are not a giddy girl whose head is easily turned. Why, you are a happily married woman."

She was right, but not entirely. True, I was not a giddy girl, my head was not easily turned. But I had grave doubts if I was still a happily married woman. In fact, I was beginning to question happiness—like Ralston questioning love—wondering what it was, if there was such a state of soul or mind. What was it really, but a handful of moments sprinkled here and there like bits of cake frosting to cover the unappetizing and sometimes bitter hours of everyday living? For now happiness seemed like an unreal luxury. I had seen a murder—my first, and I hoped my last—and because I was a witness, I was involved and I was afraid. And this awful killing, instead of drawing Adam and me together, for some reason which I could not fathom, seemed to have driven us further apart. It was no wonder happiness seemed an impossibility. I would have been well content to forget about it, never crave or want it, if only uncertainty and fear, the pain under my heart, would go away.

When we came to the cabin door Mathilda was still chatting. "I'm not going to let a thing like murder put me in the dumps. Not that I have a heart of stone, but I've seen too much senseless bloodshed in my time, and sorrowing over it doesn't seem to make any difference. My dear, take my advice, let your mind skim over it. I hate to see you so downcast."

"I cannot help it," I said. And for a moment the temptation to tell her everything was almost more than I could bear. "I would like to ask you in," I said. "But I am tired . . ."

"That's quite all right. I understand." She handed Roxanne to me. I felt that my silence, my holding back was a betrayal of our friendship. "Have a good rest," she said. "And don't worry too much."

I undressed a still sleeping Roxanne and put her to bed. Then dousing her lamp, I knelt by her side, looking down at her face in the soft light streaming in from the outer cabin. She stirred, fluttering her eyelids, mumbling something I could not catch. How much she was getting to look like me, I thought, with a sudden burst of love. And how innocent, how dear she seemed asleep. Nothing was going to happen to her—to me, to Adam. We would reach Shanghai. In the meantime I would follow Adam's instructions. And Mathilda's advice. I would try to put the killing of Ching out of my mind. It would not be easy, but there were only five days, a week at most, before we reached port. I meant to survive that week, survive to look back on it all as a bad dream, for Roxanne's sake if nothing else.

I bent to kiss her again when the cabin behind me went suddenly dark. The lamp, I thought, a cold chill creeping up my legs, the lamp was low on oil. It had not been filled for some time. Or had it?

I got up on stiff legs. The cabin was black as ink, the porthole like a darker stain against it. I stretched out my hands to feel for the wall. It was then that I caught a sound, the merest whisper of sound, an indrawn breath.

I had forgotten to lock the door. "Who is it?" I called hoarsely.

Only the creaking of the ship answered me.

"Is someone here?" I was blind, I could not see. I did not even know from which direction the sound had come. Instinctively, with clenched fists, I moved backwards into Roxanne's cubbyhole. Nothing was going to happen to her. I thought I saw a shadow glide past the doorway, and then I saw a thin bar of light, heard the click of the outer door. Groping my way across to the door I opened it, just in time to see Edith Hammersmith disappear into her cabin.

CHAPTER TEN

"Wait!" I called after her, outraged. "Wait!"

Mathilda popped her head out. "What is it?"

"Edith Hammersmith has been in my cabin."

I went boldly down to the Hammersmith's door and knocked upon it. Thomas opened up immediately. He was wearing a blue striped nightcap, the fringed tassel hanging down between his eyes. Under other circumstances the sight of him prepared for bed would have given me pause, but I was in no mood for niceties. "I want to speak to Edith," I said firmly. "Your wife."

He stepped aside and I went in. Edith was standing with her back to the bunk, clasping a book in her hand, eyeing me defiantly, yet fearfully, rather like a cornered ferret.

"What were you doing in my cabin?" I wanted to know.

"I . . ." She held out the book. "I only came to take back my book." It was a book of Sunday school stories that had entranced Roxanne, which Edith had lent us some time ago.

"I did not hear you knock and ask to come in."

"I did not think you were there. I thought you were still in the saloon, and the door was unlocked."

"So you came in without invitation?"

There was a high red color on her face. "I did not think you would mind."

"You did not see me in the adjoining cabin?"

"Why, no."

I could understand why she had not, since I had been kneeling directly under the porthole next to Roxanne's bed, out of view from anyone entering the cabin.

"And the lamp," I said. "Why did you put the lamp out?"

"Mrs. Hayworth, I didn't put the lamp out. It just went, and when you called, why . . ." She bit her lip. "I was too embarrassed to answer. I knew I was in the wrong coming in the way I did . . ." She looked at her husband appealingly with round moist eyes.

He patted her on the shoulder. "That is all right, my dear.

No harm done. It was an oversight on your part, bad manners at the worst. I'm sure Mrs. Hayworth will forgive you."

"I do apologize," said Edith humbly.

Actress? Accomplished liar? There was no way I could dispute her word. I could do nothing but swallow my anger. "In the future, please, *please* knock. My nerves . . ."

"Yes, yes," said Thomas soothingly. "I can understand. People murdered and a valuable object stolen."

A valuable object stolen. Suddenly Adam's words came back to me. "Why the hands would rip the ship apart searching for it." The hands—and the passengers, too? Yes, so many would want it, not the least of whom was Edith Hammersmith. I could not forget how she had described the idol, the avid sheen which had come to her eyes. Perhaps she had known of its existence as far back as Rainbow Creek when she had been a member of Bella Kincaid's "boarding house." Edith Hammersmith. What a price that Buddha would fetch, what a sum. More than enough to build a church and a mission school.

I went back to my cabin wondering if Edith Hammersmith had come tiptoeing through the unlocked door—and she had tiptoed, she must have, else I would have heard her—hoping to find the Buddha hidden there. Or was there another reason? I thought of her, not as the meek, little missionary's wife, quiet, subdued, shy, but as the Edith Hammersmith I had seen in Bella Kincaid's cabin, a woman who had thrust a knife under my chin. Her husband, a man of God, would never stoop to theft and murder, but Edith would. She had already killed a man, if Bella could be believed. Once done another would not matter. And she was in love with Thomas Hammersmith, in love and grateful because he had married her, giving her a respectability she had never hoped to have. She had lied to him about her past. Why not steal and kill for him too?

And I had seen her do it.

I broke into a sweat picturing her as she might have stood in the dark behind me, slowly drawing her carve-handled knife from her sleeve.

But that picture did not fit with my other one, the one I had carried with me since the night of the murder. I had watched a tall man in oilskins kill Ching, and Edith hardly came up to my shoulder. Perhaps I was accusing her of motives and deed of which she was entirely innocent.

Yet Edith's silent, furtive presence in the cabin had disturbed me and when Adam came in I began to tell him about it. I did not get very far in my narrative before he interrupted me angrily.

"I believe," he said, "my instructions to you were to keep the door locked. *Locked* at all times."

"I had not been thinking."

"Think then, Charlotte." He started to unbutton his jacket. "Use that wooden head of yours."

That stung. "I cannot be so terribly at fault if I forgot, what with so many things on my mind."

His mouth set in a grim line, he threw his jacket on the chair.

"Adam," I said, wondering how we had reached such a pass where only a few words could trigger a quarrel. "The Buddha . . . the Buddha is not the most important thing in this world. Certainly not something to come between us."

"A pox on the Buddha!" he exploded. "You still do not understand what has happened here, do you? Murder. A man is swept overboard—bad, very bad. All right. The second mate goes mad. Terrible. These, however, are things that sometimes happen at sea. It is to be expected. But murder of a passenger? And the murderer not known, not found?"

"I am very well aware of the gravity of the situation. It is just that I do not care to be scolded like a simple-minded child."

"A simple-minded child would have locked the door."

"I am sorry. It shall not happen again."

"See that it does not."

He began to undo his shirt. There was something about the set of his jaw which frightened, but at the same time angered, me.

"So I have made a mistake," I said. "I apologize."

He went on with his shirt.

"My apology seems to make no difference."

Silence.

"Perhaps you think I ought to be flogged. Well, there are plenty of ropes about, or would you prefer a cat-o-nine tails?"

He gave me a long, withering look.

"Why do you stand there and gape at me?" It was as if the devil had got hold of my tongue. "Are you mute?"

He did not answer. Throwing his jacket and shirt over his arm he strode to the door. "Lock it," he said between clenched teeth.

I stared at the closed door, anger draining to futile despair. The rift between Adam and me, starting as a small, insignificant crack when we first sailed, growing wider and wider with the passing of each day, had now become an abyss, deep, impossible to cross. I no longer had illusions about our relationship mending once we reached port. Our marriage had foundered, just as surely as if the *Duchess* had struck a reef and gone down. All the things Mother Hayward had said about me were true. I was a shopkeeper's daughter, not suited for a man of the sea. I was too spoiled, too pampered. I did not have the stiff backbone, the good breeding necessary for those who married Hayworth men. And Ralston, with his scorn, his curling lip, had been right from the very start. "Captains' wives should remain at home."

The fact that I still loved Adam, loved him in a sick, hopeless way, did not matter. I had come on this voyage, happy, buoyant, thinking—how foolishly—it was to be our second honeymoon, that we would be together, sharing the good and the bad, that our love would grow, deepen. But now I knew Adam did not love me. Our good times in that small house on Beacon Street had been a passing thing for him, a sailor enjoying his pleasure in port. What I had thought was happiness, contentment, as love for myself as a person, was not love. It was just that he was a man and I was his wife, a young woman, and he lived for long periods in a world without women. His real love, his only love was the sea and *The Secret Duchess* who was intrinsically bound up with it. He did not belong to me at all. He belonged to a mistress, fickle, beguiling, angry, beautiful, exciting.

It was strange too, looking back, that my agony, my sick despair, overshadowed the principal reason for our quarrel—Sam Ching's murder. I remember waking the next morning more fearful lest the passengers know Adam had not shared my bed, than that somewhere, close by, perhaps, was someone, a murderer, whom I did not know but who knew me.

On the night following the quarrel I was sitting in the chair trying to read when there was a knock on the door. "Mrs. Hayworth?" a voice I recognized as the bosun's inquired, "are you awake?"

"Yes, Mr. Phipps. What is it?" I asked through the closed door.

"A man's been badly hurt below. He was splicing a rope and he cut himself. The captain said you had bandages . . ."

"Yes, yes, I am coming."

I got the box of medicines, took a quick look at Roxanne, then went out, locking the door behind me. "Where is he?"

" 'Tween decks," he said. "He is one of the foremast hands. But the captain says you are to bring Mrs. Jackson with you."

Well, I thought, at least, if nothing else, he is still concerned for my safety.

I knocked on Mathilda's door. "Are you up?" I whispered.

She answered at once, and when I explained what had happened she threw a shawl over her shoulders and joined us.

The man was lying in a hammock with a deep gash running from his thumb across the palm of his hand. I tied his wrist tightly, trying to stem the flow of blood. However, the bandage soon soaked through.

"That won't do," said Mathilda. "I have an old flannel nightgown that's much more absorbent. Let me fetch it. I'll be back in a minute."

The young sailor's face had gone a pasty white, and I feared he would faint. "Are you in great pain?" I asked.

He tried to smile, a pathetic grimace. "A wee bit."

I had some laudanum and I asked the bosun to get me a spoon.

"Some grog would be better," he said. "That stuff, beggin' your pardon, ma'am, will do for women or babies, but not for Johnnie here."

He came back in a few minutes with a bottle and, lifting the injured man's head, put it to his lips.

"Ah," said Johnnie, a tinge of color returning to his cheeks.

"Better is it, John boy?" Mr. Phipps got to his feet. "If you will pardon me, Mrs. Hayworth, but it's my watch."

"Of course," I said.

The blood had seeped through Johnnie's bandage, and I replaced it with another. In a minute it had turned pale pink, but no more. "I think we have the bleeding stopped," I said. "In the morning I will put a clean dressing on. Meanwhile I would suggest you not use that hand."

"I don't think I could if I tried, ma'am. And thank you."

"It is quite all right." I repacked the medicine kit.

Mathilda had not yet returned. Perhaps, I thought, she could not find the flannel nightgown. Concerned about leaving Roxanne alone for so long, I decided to go back, feeling sure I would meet Mathilda on the way.

'Tween decks was dimly lit, and for a few moments I felt turned around and uncertain which way I had come. "The ladder is straight ahead," Johnnie said, pointing.

My feet made a hollow sound in the darkness. I had gone a little distance when I paused, peering ahead, wondering if I had heard Johnnie correctly, for I could not see the ladder. Then my eyes, having grown accustomed to the darkness, perceived it some yards away.

I had taken only a few steps when I felt something nudge my shoulder, and I stumbled.

Suddenly the bottom literally dropped from under my feet, and I was falling, plummeting into an eternity of black space. The wind knocked out of me, my mind a screaming, gaping horror, my hands thrashed about, clawing, grasping. It was like a bad dream, one of those horrible nightmares in which one falls endlessly. Rope burned and slithered in and out of my desperate fingers. My knee caught briefly—then I was falling again.

Finally, unbelievably, a thousand years later, I hit bottom with a shattering thud. When I could collect my rocketing senses I discovered I was resting on something soft and hairy, surrounded by complete darkness. Every bone in my body ached, every muscle cried out in pain. I was certain I had been broken, fragmented down to my very toes. I moved first one arm, then the other. I did the same with my legs. They seemed whole.

Painfully, I pushed myself into a sitting position. A rank, rotting odor, clung to my nostrils, choking my lungs. I moved my hand slowly, tentatively around. The soft, hairy substance on which I rested was a fur. The uncrated furs . . . I had fallen into the hold!

Another stupidity was my first thought; Adam will have reason again to scold. I had stumbled in clumsy, unheeding fashion into an open hatch or ventilator. I looked up, but there was no hole, no opening. My straining eyes circled the darkness. Nothing. I could not even see the ladder which had apparently broken my fall. I sat for a few minutes frowning. And it came to me suddenly as a bright light stabbing the gloom. The hatch cover had been replaced after my fall. That could only mean one thing. The cover had not been carelessly left open, no more than the unseen object which had bumped my shoulders was accidental. Someone had opened the hatch, someone who had been watching, waiting in the shadows for me. Then I had been deliberately pushed. Were it not for the impeding ladder and the furs which had cushioned my fall I should be lying now with a broken neck, quite possibly dead.

The thought brought a rising panic to my throat and I opened my mouth to scream. But reason caught me before I could make more than a gargled sound. I suddenly realized that whoever had contrived my "accident" might still be hanging about, waiting to hear if I still lived.

I bit my lip hard, hard, trying to hold to rational thought.

I must not utter a sound. Patience, I told myself, patience. Sooner or later I would be missed. Mathilda! I remembered with sudden relief. She would return to the injured man with her flannel nightgown and, not finding me, would raise an alarm. She and Mr. Phipps and some of the others would search and eventually discover me in the hold. It was reasonable. Very reasonable. I sat there hugging my shoulders against the foul, chill air.

It was dark in the hold, but it was not silent. There was the constant swish-swish, a gurgling of water, bilge, I thought, and an intermittent nibbling, gnawing sound. The scurrying of small feet. Small . . .

Rats! The rats who would leave a sinking ship. And because I could not see the ugly, loathsome creatures, my sick fear increased. The nausea which I had been fighting for some time rose in a lump to my mouth and I retched. Unpleasant as it was, it kept me again from screaming, from panic.

I shifted my position, tucking my legs under me and drew in my skirts, wrapping them about me tightly as if within them I could find shelter. I sat there hardly daring to breath, my eyes bulging in the darkness, imagining a dozen pairs of beady eyes upon me, a ring of small, whiskered snouts twitching. There was a slight tug at my skirt, a nibble, and before I could move one of the unseen, horrid creatures scurried across my lap. I sprang to my feet and screamed.

I began to stumble about blindly, in jibbering terror, searching for the ladder. My knees knocked against a crate and I fell across it. I lay there for a moment, sobbing, blubbering like a witless idiot. My hands went over the splintered boards and closed on an iron bar. I picked it up and began to pound on the crate, shouting hysterically all the while.

My God, I thought, even in the midst of frantic despair, they will think it is mad Mr. Griggs knocking and screaming and thrashing about in his confinement. I had to find the ladder.

Still clutching the bar—at least it would serve as a weapon against the hungry, ravenous rats—I got to my feet. Think, think. When I fell I must have come down in a direct line from the hatch, landing on the furs. I had made a foolish mistake, one more to add to the other. I should never have moved from that nest of furs. I felt my way across the floor with the bar, like a blind man using a cane, and suddenly the bar touched something soft and yielding. A tiny squeal. Without thinking I lifted the bar and brought it down again and again, unseeing, while the creature continued to squeal. I kept on with the blows, angry, desperate, possessed of a fury that can only come from stark terror. I went on hitting the soft mass at my feet long after it had ceased to make a sound.

Finally, when I came to my senses, I realized if I went on in this manner I should soon have no senses to come to. The rats were there. I could not kill the whole population. The quicker I got out of the hold the better. I began my sightless search again.

A few minutes later I was rewarded by the sound of iron ringing against iron. The ladder. I dropped the bar and, hoisting my skirts to my hips, began to climb. It was slow going, since my gown kept slipping and I had to use both hands for climbing. Hand over hand I went, testing each step with my foot, not daring to think what would happen should I slip and fall again. The rungs went on and on, seemingly into infinity. My legs and arms developed new, agonizing aches, but my mind kept moving, urging them upward.

My throat was now raw, my breath like a knife in my chest. When it seemed I had not the strength to make one more step, I paused, clinging to the ladder, listening to the sound of my heavy breathing.

Then I heard something else. Above. I lifted my head. Footsteps, the murmur of voices.

"Help!" I shouted hoarsely. "It's Charlotte! Help!"

The voices came closer. A grating, a clanking, and the hatch cover was lifted with a sweet rush of giddy air. A face, then another and another, featureless faces, all peering down at me. A lantern was thrust into the opening, its beam shattering my vision.

"Why, it is Mrs. Hayworth!" I heard Mathilda's shocked voice exclaim. Strong arms reached down and pulled me up as if I were a rag doll.

Someone helped me to my feet. "How in the world did you get down there?" Mr. Phipps asked, his watery eyes popping incredulously in the lantern light.

"I fell . . ." My knees buckled and Mathilda Jackson put her arm around me.

"My dear," she said, "we have been searching the place over. I was just going to ask the captain to stop the ship since I was afraid you'd fallen overboard."

"No . . . the hatch was open."

The bosun scratched his head. "I can't see how that was, m'am. The hatches are never opened at night."

"But I was . . ." I tried to explain.

Mathilda said, "Come along, Charlotte. You are in no condition to argue with the bosun here. And Mr. Phipps, see if you can't bring up a pot of strong tea for the captain's wife."

"Yes . . . yes, ma'am."

I leaned heavily on Mathilda as we made our way across the deck. "You might have been killed," she said. "My God, when I think of it." Her arm tightened about me, her strength flowing through me like balm.

When we reached the cabin, she made me sit while she got a wet towel and washed the grime from my face. I caught a glimpse of myself in the mirror: tangled hair straggling down past my shoulders, dirty, smudged tear streaks across my cheeks, and my eyes, so enormous, still hollow with my awful fear. "There were rats down there," I said and shuddered. "Thousands."

"You poor baby," said Mathilda, hugging me.

Hot tears rose to my eyes. "I was pushed," I said. "Someone pushed me."

"*Pushed* you? What do you mean?"

"I am sure I was pushed. I felt something on my shoulders and I pitched forward then . . . straight down. Lucky for me I fell on a pile of furs."

"Why should anyone do a thing like that?" There was a faint hint of doubt in her voice.

"Because I saw Sam Ching killed." There it was—out. I did not care any longer that Adam had warned me to keep silent. I had to tell someone, someone who would give me a kind word, sympathy.

"But, Charlotte . . ."

"You do not believe me. You think I got a knock on the head when I fell into the hold, and it has made me daft. I got knocked all over: on the head, on the arms, the legs, and the small of my back hurts. But I never fainted, and I never let completely go of my wits. I tell you I was pushed."

There was a look of deep concern in her eyes, but she said nothing.

"All right," I went on. "For the sake of argument suppose I was not pushed, maybe I just thought I was. But I did not imagine seeing someone stab Sam Ching."

"Charlotte, dear, if you *saw* who did it, why didn't you come forward?"

"I saw a man in oilskins. It was too dark to see anything but the shape of him. I don't know who it was. I tried to run and he hit me before I could get out into the passage.

Adam found me later. Sam Ching was dead and the Buddha . . ."

"The Buddha?"

"Yes, Mathilda, both Edith and Bella were right. The Celestial Buddha exists and Sam Ching had it. Adam made me promise not to say anything. He said the murderer could not be sure I hadn't recognized him and it was dangerous . . ."

"And you think the man in oilskins was the one who pushed you?"

"I can find no other reason for that open hatch. You heard Mr. Phipps say it was kept closed at night."

"Yes. Oh, my dear, that is so dreadful!"

It was on the tip of my tongue to tell her how cross Adam had been with me to have become entangled in a murder—although unwittingly—and how angry he was with me all the time now. But I could not. That my marriage was a sham, I could tell no one.

"You poor dear," she said, holding me to her for a few moments. "I never dreamed . . . And to think I did not stay with you. If I had only known."

Just then Mr. Phipps rapped at the door with our tea, apologizing for taking so long. Mathilda thanked him and poured me a cup and one for herself. It was hot and strong.

"I should have come back at once," said Mathilda. "Not left you alone. If I had been with you, no one would have dared to push us *both* into the hold."

"I waited a good while," I said. "I thought I might meet you on the way. Did something happen?"

She stirred her tea with a spoon. "I didn't want to tell you for fear of upsetting you even more. But when I got to my cabin it was a shambles. Someone had been searching through it. Drawers pulled out, my clothes all over the bunk and floor."

"Someone looking for the Celestial Buddha," I said.

"Now that you've told me there's one and that it was stolen, I suppose that was it."

"Who?"

"Stands to reason it wasn't the murderer. He *has* it."

"Adam said once the word got out the hands would be looking for it."

"Hmmmm."

We drank our tea in silence.

Mathilda pursed her lips. "You say it was a tall man you saw stabbing Sam Ching?"

"Yes, a tall man in oilskins."

"Hmmmn. Barring someone in the crew . . ." She stirred her tea again. "If I were to guess, and mind you it is only a guess, I don't want to go putting my finger on an innocent man, but . . . if I was to guess it would come mighty close to Thomas Hammersmith."

I looked at her in amazement. "But he did not know about the Buddha."

"Edith might have told him. You heard her story. I'd say she didn't tell the whole of it. She had a funny look in her eye."

"But Mr. Hammersmith, a man of God?"

"Well, what of it? I ain't an educated woman, Charlotte, but I've read a bit in my time. And there's been more killing in the name of holiness than those who carried the cross would want to admit. From the Crusades to those poor heathens in the New World who was burned and knifed and garroted because they wouldn't bend their knees. All for a good cause, mind you. And whatever cause would be more sanctified than getting the wherewithal to build a church and mission school?"

It was exactly what I had thought of Edith Hammersmith. And I had dismissed her because she was a woman and far too short. The person who had killed Sam Ching was tall. Like Mr. Hammersmith.

CHAPTER ELEVEN

I would have preferred to keep my tumble into the hold from Adam, since I had expressly gone against his instructions by crossing the deck alone, and at night. I might have even lied about those bruises on my arms, and the ugly purple bump on my forehead. But like anything else that happened on the ship, my misadventure was a matter of common knowledge within hours. Fortunately, Mathilda had said nothing about our subsequent conversation, and so Adam thought like the others it had been an accident. Nevertheless it was bad enough.

He vented his anger by not speaking to me at all, the worst sort of punishment he could have devised. Though Adam had come back to our bed, it was like sleeping with a corpse. One morning, two days after my experience in the hold, I lay on the bunk, watching as he silently finished shaving. He rinsed the lather from his face, toweled it, threw the towel on the washstand and got into his shirt, all without a word or a glance in my direction. Unable to bear the strained silence between us another moment I said, "Are we to go on this way, not speaking?"

He turned, his eyes, tired and strained, resting on me. "I have to be angry with you sometimes, Charlotte."

"Yes, I know I have not always been a model wife," I said, thinking guiltily of all the promises I had broken since Ching had been killed, "but in the future I shall try to do better."

He stared at me moodily. "I wonder if I did a very selfish thing in bringing you."

I felt cold, rather sick. "You regret it?"

He sighed and reached for his jacket. "I'm afraid it is too late for regrets."

"Too late?" My throat felt dry and hot, my eyes were burning. I expected he would say that some day. Yet I had hoped against hope. . . . "Why is it too late?"

He looked at me again, and it seemed there were words struggling within him, words he found difficult to utter.

"What is it, Adam? Do you want Roxanne and me to go home? We can, you know. When we get to Shanghai we can take a ship back to San Francisco. Would that make you happy?"

"Don't talk nonsense, Charlotte," he said wearily.

Roxanne came in from her cubbyhole, tousled and sleepy-eyed. "Papa . . ."

He picked her up and kissed her. "Papa, stay with me and play cat's cradle," she said, winding her small arms about his neck.

"Not now, darling." He kissed her again and set her on her feet. "Later perhaps."

I had not been out of the cabin since my mishap. To Mathilda, who had called twice, I had given my bruised face as an excuse, but the truth was I was too miserably depressed to want anyone's company. After Adam left I spent the morning trying to amuse Roxanne, who chafed more and more under our confinement. She got very silly, laughing and squealing at the slightest provocation, and it taxed my powers of restraint not to smack her and order her to bed. Poor darling. She was hardly to blame for our troubles and certainly not for the gulf between Adam and me.

When luncheon was over and the steward had removed our tray, Roxanne seemed to quiet down, playing with her rag dolly, talking to it and pretending to give it tea on her bunk. I dropped wearily into the chair under the porthole, exhausted to the marrow, feeling a thousand years old, though my twenty-fifth birthday was only a month away. I had lain awake most of the night, stiff and silent next to Adam, my mind going in circles like a ploughing donkey on a treadmill, asking myself a thousand questions over and over. It seemed years since I had had a night's decent, unbroken sleep.

I picked up a book, but I was too tired to open it and sat there, my eyes staring dully at the morocco-bound cover, the title in gilt letters, *The Three Clerks*. I must have read that book in its entirety sometime during the long voyage, goodness knows there were enough idle hours for the reading of twenty novels, but what this one was about, who the characters were, where it took place, I have not the vaguest memory.

It was hot and stuffy in the cabin. I really must take Roxanne out for a stroll, I thought; it is not fair to keep her caged up simply because I am trying to hide. Somewhere a fly hummed and buzzed. My eyelids grew heavy. I slept.

When I awoke a band of dust-moted sun was slanting

through the porthole. The fly had vanished. It was very quiet in the cabin; even the pitch and creak of the ship seemed muted. Roxanne, I thought, stretching my sore arms, must have fallen asleep too.

I got up slowly, stretching again, and peeked in her door. There was no sleeping Roxanne. Her doll was there, the little scraps of cloth laid out on the pillow, the tiny china cups, but no sign of Roxanne. I looked behind the door. "Roxanne?" She sometimes hid there or in the cupboard as a sort of game. But she was not behind the door nor was she in the cupboard.

My heart dropped to my shoes. If something should happen to Roxanne . . . For anything else I could, I might, forgive myself, but never for falling alseep and allowing harm to come to Roxanne. I rushed through the door and ran out on deck, colliding with a sailor. "Have you seen my little girl?" I asked.

"Why, no . . . no, ma'am."

"Please," I implored. "You must help me find her. She . . ." Without waiting for an answer I ran to the rail. It was too high for her, but she might, if she stood on a coil of rope, reach it. I looked over the side. The wake of the ship was a white line in the tea green water. Water which went down to bottomless depths where finned monsters . . . "No," I whispered, gripping the rail, "no, no." Surely someone would have seen and stopped her if she had been climbing the rail?

"Ma'am," the sailor said behind me. "Have you tried the galley?"

"The . . . galley . . . thank you." I dashed down to the galley. Roxanne liked the galley. Several times we had stopped there during our excursions on deck, and Cookie had given her a sweet.

She was not in the galley.

One of the cabins? In my haste I had forgotten to look. She might have gone in to visit with Mathilda. I ran back across the deck, my mind flying ahead of me, hoping I would find her before Adam knew she was missing. No one answered my knock and the door, when I tried it, was fastened. Perhaps they were in the saloon. Mathilda often went there of an afternoon to think or to knit. She did not like to be cooped up all day in her cabin. Back I went and down the stairs to the saloon. Empty. The table ringed by eight, stark chairs, the lounge seat looking more faded in the semi-gloom. Only a fly, a single one, the same one I was sure which had visited me earlier, buzzed at the porthole window.

I flew back up the stairs. Roxanne had been kidnapped. The murderer had snatched her away and was holding her hostage. The ransom, my silence, a ransom which I would gladly pay. But I did not know *who* the murderer was. I did not know. And somehow he had managed to unlock my door while I was asleep. I pictured him (still incongruously in oilskins, because that was the way I had seen him) stealing past my sleeping figure into Roxanne's cubbyhole, clapping a rough hairy hand over her mouth, and dragging her, struggling and kicking, from the bunk.

The murderer. Thomas Hammersmith? Yes. It was he. Mathilda Jackson thought so. And there was a church to build and a school. It must be the preacher. When I got to his cabin, I flung open the door without pausing to knock. Thomas was sitting in a chair, his trousers rolled up, soaking his feet in a basin of water. His mouth flew open, his face turning a deep red at the sight of me.

"Roxanne! Where is she?" I looked about me wildly.

His mouth still hung open. He blinked his eyes. Edith emerged from behind the screen, carrying a towel. "What is it?" she asked.

"Roxanne . . . I want to know where she is!"

They both stared at me dumbly.

"Well—what did you do with her?"

They continued to stare.

Again I looked around. The cabin, smaller than ours, was neat as a pin. Everything was in its place, the bunk tidily made up, the dressing table bare except of a Bible, and hanging from pegs, a cloak and a suit of oilskins. No Roxanne. There was not a place in that small cabin where they could possibly hide her, unless they stuffed her in a drawer or chucked her out the porthole.

"Mrs. Hayworth," Thomas spoke at last, "this is embarrassing, to say the least. My wife . . . Edith was . . . I have this painful inflammation of the feet and . . . and . . . very embarrassing."

It was the first time I had known Thomas Hammersmith to be at a loss for words. And somehow the sight of him, bereft of his usual pomposity, his bare, skinny legs stuck into the basin, his hair rumpled and his nose red, cleared my head. Never, as I looked at him now, could I imagine him a murderer.

"I am sorry," I apologized, "but Roxanne is gone. And I am half out of my head with worry."

"Yes, yes, I quite understand," said Mr. Hammersmith,

lifting one dripping foot from the basin. Edith quickly knelt and dried it.

"We shall be happy to help you look for her at once," he said earnestly. "Where are my socks, dearest?"

"I'll get them in a moment. Your other foot?" He raised it and she applied the towel.

He bent suddenly and brushed a curl from her forehead; she looked up at him with such naked love in her eyes, I had to turn my own away. They loved one another, these two, not passionately, perhaps, but it was a love I envied. Then and there I forgave Edith for her hardness toward me, for her threats, once made it seemed in the long, long ago. How, I asked myself silently could either of these two have killed anyone in cold blood for monetary gain? I was not so sure of that any more.

As Thomas Hammersmith was pulling on his socks, I heard a peal of high, merry laughter. Roxanne! I could never mistake that laugh. I was out the door in a wink. The laughter again. It came from Bella Kincaid's cabin.

This time I had the presence of mind to knock. "Come in," Bella's raspy contralto called.

Roxanne, seated cross-legged on the bunk, was gazing raptly at Bella who was wearing an enormous plumed hat and preening herself at the mirror. "Mama!" Roxanne exclaimed. "Mrs. Kincaid has the funniest hats."

"Where have you been?" I demanded, the first moment of relief replaced by anger. I went to her and took her roughly by the hand. "Have you any idea the grief, the worry, you have caused me?"

"Why no, Mama," she replied innocently. "You were sleeping, and I did not think you would mind."

"I do mind. I *did* mind. I have been all over the ship. If your father only knew he would be so angry. You have been very, very naughty."

Roxanne's large green-brown eyes filled with tears, and her lower lip stuck out.

"Don't scold her, Charlotte," Bella said. "I invited her in. I should have sent her back, but she said you were resting, and we've had so much fun together. What's the harm in that?"

"None, I suppose, but . . ." Now that it was over and Roxanne found, my panic seemed slightly ridiculous. On the other hand, I reminded myself, a murder had been done on *The Secret Duchess,* and I had every right to be fearful of

Roxanne's safety. ". . . but she is too small to go wandering about."

"She may be small," said Bella, "but she is a bright young thing, and I think very able to take care of herself."

"Oh?" I resented her giving me advice, no matter how obliquely, on how to rear my child. Women who had never had any of their own were always full of counsel, and it galled me to listen to these pearls of wisdom, especially from someone like Bella. "What Roxanne is able or not able to do is for me to decide."

"You needn't get snippy about it," said Bella. "I wasn't planning to gobble her whole."

"Can't I stay a bit longer?" Roxanne pleaded. "Mrs. Kincaid is showing me her hats."

Bella said, "That's right. I have quite a collection."

"I do not think . . ."

"Come now, Charlotte, don't be a spoil sport," Bella chided. "Sit down and join my audience. Just because the Chinaman . . ."

"There is no need for that," I warned. Roxanne, of course, knew nothing of the horrible tragedy. And I did not see why she had to know.

"Please, Mama," Roxanne begged.

"Well . . . all right then. Just for a few minutes." I sat down beside Roxanne.

The room was close, reeking of perfume and stale gin. Bella removed the plumed hat and put it aside. Then from a large box at her feet she took an impertinent, little flat "porkpie" hat, tufted at the side with a delicate egret feather. When she placed it atop her head, Roxanne shouted with glee. Bella's flushed, pendulous face looked quite absurd beneath it. "It's not exactly my style," said Bella, twisting her face this way and that before the mirror, "but I tell you it is the latest, the very latest from Paris."

I wondered, if like her necklace, a count had given it to her. But no, for she was saying, "I bought it from one of my girls." Here she winked at me. "She was French and had brought it over with her and needed the money." She sighed and removed the hat.

"And this," she said, reaching into the box, drawing out a faded lavender bonnet embellished with a drooping spray of cloth violets, "this, was my granny's. Would you believe I had a granny? I did, my dear," she said, nodding at Roxanne. She got up from the chair, pushing the box aside, and placed the bonnet on Roxanne's head, tying it under the chin. It was much too big, of course, the brim flopping down over her eyes.

"I want to see!" Roxanne cried, wiggling herself off the bunk.

"Come look in the mirror," Bella invited.

Roxanne was in raptures. She thought she looked quite elegant. Bella went to a cupboard and got a bright, garish purple shawl and threw it around Roxanne's shoulders, sending her into spasms of "ohs" and "ahs."

I had to admit that Bella had a way with children. Perhaps she was not such a bad sort after all. Or so I thought until I happened to glance down at the box. There at the bottom, under a jumble of hats, something shiny was peeking through. It looked like an oilskin sou'wester, but I could not be sure. I had my hand out to reach for it when Bella turned.

"Now what do you think of your little one?" she asked.

"Lovely. You look lovely, Roxanne." But I was not thinking of Roxanne. I was thinking of that shiny piece at the bottom of the box. For directly across from me on a hook was another sou'wester and an oilskin, the regular ones each of us had been provided with, and a terrible suspicion began to gnaw at me. Sou'westers were not the sort of headgear a woman would collect, not even Bella. "May I look through your hats?" I asked casually. "There are some pretty ones."

"Oh, not *there*," she said. "There's nothing but my old ones left. My new ones, the best ones I keep in the cupboard. I'll show you."

So I had to leave the box and go to the cupboard with Bella and pretend an interest in a velvet toque and a lace frilled bonnet. I was itching to get my fingers into that pile of old hats, but there was no way of doing it, nor any way of satisfying my curiosity short of asking Bella point-blank if she owned two oilskin hats. That I could not do.

Later in the afternoon as I strolled the deck with Roxanne, I kept thinking of the hat and asking myself why I should attach so much importance to it. I was not even sure it *was* a hat. Besides the murderer had been a man.

Or had it been?

I stopped so suddenly, Roxanne, who had hold of my hand, was jerked backward. "What is it, Mama?" she asked.

"Nothing," I said, and we continued our stroll.

Of course it did not have to be a man. The oilskins came almost to the floor with only the tips of shoes showing. The hat had been pulled low. Underneath it there would have been either a man or a woman. For the dozenth time I pictured

Sam Ching's cabin, the lamp on the floor, the moving, tall shadow on the wall. Had my terrified mind exaggerated the height?

Bella Kincaid was not very tall; on the other hand, neither was she short. It was she who had come out at the very first and flatly stated Sam Ching possessed the Celestial Buddha. Would she have done so if she were the guilty party? She was shrewd, Mathilda had said. What better way to divert any hint of suspicion from herself than to boldly tell her story, especially since I knew she had been at Rainbow Creek? I thought of the string of pearls over which she had made such a fuss, her "stake" she had called it, a string of pearls with the clasp turned green. Those pearls could not have been worth very much. However, if she could get the Buddha, she would never have to worry about "fending" for herself again.

But how would she have known this was the same Ching? Ching was a common enough name. Perhaps, from the description of the ghostly yellow glove, she had guessed.

Just as I was guessing now, I told myself ruefully.

Still the shiny bit of material at the bottom of the hatbox deviled me. Somehow I had to get into Bella Kincaid's cabin when she was not there and see for myself. Adam had instructed all the passengers to keep their doors locked. But knowing Bella's laxness, there was a very good chance she rarely remembered to do this.

That night we had dinner served to us in the cabin again. As soon as Roxanne was fed, I tucked her into her bunk. She had had an exhausting day, what with being entertained by Bella and running and skipping about the rest of the afternoon on deck, and she fell asleep without reminding me she hadn't said her prayers.

Feeling like a thief, I stole down the alleyway to Bella's door. A twist of the knob showed me I had surmised correctly. The door was unlocked. I let myself in quietly. The box of hats was where Bella had left it. I went down on my knees and began to paw through the bonnets and porkpies and straw skimmers. It was there at the bottom. An oilskin hat. But there was more: the oilskins themselves, with dark, splattered stains down the front.

My heart was beating in a wild, eerie way. Careless Bella, not to have thrown them overboard or hidden them more cleverly. Careless of Adam and Ralston, too, not to have found them.

I began to look for the Buddha. I did not have to worry about tidying up as I went through the cupboards. Everything was such a mess anyway. Perhaps it had been this very fact which had confused Adam and prevented him from making a thorough search. I shook out petticoats and peered into shoe boxes and undid two portmanteaux. I pulled out every drawer, those under the bunk and in the dressing table. I found dirty linen aplenty plus a half dozen empty gin bottles and several newspapers of the same issue giving an account of Mother Belle's trial. But no Buddha.

Its absence did not mean she had not killed Sam Ching. Frightened, she might have fled after knocking me unconscious, and someone else, seeing the open door, had come in and stolen the idol. I picked up the oilskin coat and threw it around my shoulders to gauge the length. It was long, all right. I was slightly taller than Bella and it reached nearly to the floor. Next I tried the hat.

I was looking in the mirror when I saw the door open. I whirled about.

Bella Kincaid was standing on the threshold, her eyes wide with shock.

CHAPTER TWELVE

She clutched at the door handle, her face white as paper, the painted cheeks standing out like clown patches. My first thought was that, seeing me in the incriminating oilskins, she realized she had been discovered.

I took a step toward her; she turned and fled, shouting at the top of her lungs, "Thief! Thief!"

Feeling very much the fool, I quickly slipped out of the oilskins and hurried after her. By the time I reached the deck a small knot of people had gathered around her, some of the crew, the Hammersmiths and Mathilda. Thankfully Adam or Ralston was not among them. Bella was gesticulating wildly, her loud, excited speech making very little sense. I managed to squeeze through and grab her arm. "Bella," I said in her ear. "I know who it was."

"Who? Who?" she shouted.

"Please do not say a word and come with me," I whispered like a conspirator.

She gaped at me.

"I will take care of Mrs. Kincaid," I said to the little crowd. I held on to her arm and guided her back to the cabin.

"I have some brandy," I said to her. "If you wait a moment I shall fetch it."

She was waiting for me, sitting on a chair, nervously twisting a mug in her hands. I poured her a drink, and she took it down in one long, convulsive gulp. She held out the mug, and I emptied the bottle into it. She drank again, more slowly, and the color flowed back to her face. "My pearls," she said when the drink had settled. "I must see if my pearls are here."

I did not say anything. I was too busy trying to work out a way to explain my presence at her mirror in oilskins.

I watched as she scrabbled through the jumble on the dressing table. "Ah, here they are. I must have frightened the man away." Then turning to me, "You said you knew who it was. You saw him?"

"Why, yes." The oilskins were still on the bunk where I had tossed them. "It was me."

For a few seconds she gazed at me in astonishment. Then she began to laugh.

I picked up the oilskins. "I found these in your box of hats. I was trying them on."

"Whatever for?" she asked.

"Did you know you had two sets?" I pointed to the oilskins hanging from the peg.

She looked from me to the wall, her eyes twinkling with humor, the kind of humor one graciously bestows on a dimwit. "No. I had no idea. Why should I have two?"

"I don't know," I said. Was her innocence genuine?

"There's something that smells about this, Charlotte." Her eyes rested on me, and I could tell she was no longer amused. "Why did you come in here while I was at dinner? And where did you find those oilskins?"

So I told her the truth, or nearly the truth, since I made no mention of myself as witness to Ching's murder. "It is rumored that the person who killed Ching was wearing oilskins, and this morning when you were showing us the hats ... I thought ... you see ... you see, I was not sure ..." I stumbled on, her eyes kept staring at me, staring and growing larger. "I . . . I thought I would come back to see."

"To see what?"

"These oilskins . . . they seemed stained with . . . with blood."

She reached over and took the bottle from my hand, shaking the last few drops from it. "If that doesn't beat the devil. So you think I murdered Sam Ching, is that it?"

"Well . . . not exactly," I equivocated. "I could not understand why you should have these."

"Neither do I. Unless . . ." Her eyes narrowed. ". . . unless all you've been telling me is a damned lie. You might have come into my cabin with that rain gear to hide your own guilt."

"No, no. I found them here, I tell you. Would I be standing in front of the mirror trying them on, if I did not?"

She shrugged. "So you thought I killed the Chinaman," she repeated. She leaned over and tapped me on the knee with her ringed fingers. "I have done many things in my life. You would not believe some of them. But murder? Never."

"I am sorry," I murmured.

"Now mind you, I wouldn't balk at stealing the Buddha if I had half the chance. But knifing for it?" She shook her head.

She fell silent, and I watched her as she stared into space. "All gold . . . and studded with jewels. It would be a temptation. But . . ." She shook herself. "No . . . that's not my way. I've gotten my jewels, my gold, by loving a man, not killing him." She gave me a knowing smile.

"How do you think the oilskins got into your box?" I asked.

"Why, someone must have put them there. How else? I don't always remember to lock my door, though I suppose I should."

"Have you any idea who might have put them there?"

"Edith," she said without hesitation. "She'd like nothing better than to see me accused of murder. That girl *hates* me."

"You are not implying she killed Ching?"

"Why not? You heard her describe the Buddha, didn't you? 'Rubies red as blood.' And you saw the knife she carries."

"I do not think it was Edith," I said.

"Either her or that sanctified husband of hers."

"Not Mr. Hammersmith." A sudden vision of Thomas soaking his feet in the basin rose before me. "He is so . . ."

"Holy? Bosh. I could tell you a tale or two about preachers. I have had more than one in my parlor."

Adam came in at midnight. It struck me suddenly how thin his face had become, all angles and sharp lines and how the little frown over his nose had become permanent. "What was the Kincaid woman bellowing about this evening?" he asked.

It was on the tip of my tongue to say I had discovered the murderer's oilskins in her hat box, but then he would want to know why I was poking about in the passengers' cabins and it would raise another quarrel or another wall of silence between us, neither of which I could face. "She thought there was a thief in her cabin."

"That woman is a great one for theatrics." He sat down and lit a cigar. "I won't be unhappy to see her leave." He leaned back in his chair with the cigar between his teeth.

"Adam," I said, a little hesitantly, "Adam, did you ever think Thomas Hammersmith might have killed Ching? You know he is without funds and, well, the Buddha is worth a great deal of money, and . . ."

He threw me a sharp look. "Yes, I have thought of him. I have thought of every damned soul on this ship. Why do you ask?"

"It was a tall man, I saw. And Thomas Hammersmith is tall."

"So are a half dozen, if not more, men on the *Duchess*. But Hammersmith—no."

"Why do you say that?"

"Have you ever noticed the preacher's right arm? He moves it rather stiffly."

I thought for a moment. "Why . . . yes. Now that you mention it."

"I asked him about it immediately after the murder. His arm had been broken when he fell out of a tree as a boy. It never mended properly. Whoever killed Ching had a good strong right arm. Believe me, the knife wounds attested to that."

"So it could not have been a woman?"

"I rather doubt it." He tamped out his cigar and began to undress. When he got into bed he said, "Charlotte, why don't you let me worry about these things? Just take care of yourself and Roxanne. My only wish now is to get the ship to port without another mishap."

"But Adam . . ."

"Go to sleep, Charlotte."

Go to sleep, Charlotte. Sit, Charlotte. Stay, Charlotte. Was I no better than a pet, caressed when I was good, shouted at when I misbehaved? No, I must not think that. It was weak of me, self-pitying. Adam had too much on his mind, too many burdens to carry. Yet I would have gladly shared all of them. I wanted so much to be his wife, truly his wife and companion. Not this woman, rather foolish, rather headstrong who must be guided and instructed like a child.

As I lay there in the dark, I went into a fantasy wherein I found the murderer and recovered the Celestial Buddha. I —alone—stalwart, courageous, clever Charlotte. And the gratitude in Adam's eyes was my reward, his voice full of love and pride saying, "I am the luckiest fellow in the world to have such a wife." On that happy note I fell into a dreamless sleep. But in the morning, with Adam gone from my side, the old anxieties, the old uncertainties returned, and with them came an overwhelming sense of guilt. I had practiced a terrible deceit on Adam by withholding knowledge of the oilskins. Because I was a coward, afraid to face his anger, I had hedged—if not lied—about a crucial matter. Those oilskins could be an important link to the murderer.

I had to get to Adam before Bella did if I were to repair some of the damage of my omission. But I was too late. Not that Bella spoke to Adam; but she did to several others the night before, to the Hammersmiths, to Mathilda, to Mr.

Phipps, the bosun, and whoever else would listen to her, so that when Adam came up to the poop in the morning Ralston gave him the news.

I got another raking over the coals, exactly as I thought I would. But this time I held my tongue, answering only, "Yes, Adam," "No, Adam," "I'm sorry, Adam." It made me feel rather like a between-maid who must silently endure a dressing down for breaking a piece of china lest she lose her place. But it takes two to quarrel and that much I could spare myself.

Late that afternoon Mathilda and I were sitting in my cabin mulling over the reason why the oilskins had found their way into Bella Kincaid's hat box. "I cannot think why the murderer did not throw them overboard," I said, "as he must have done with the knife, since it was never found."

"Probably he was afraid the oilskins wouldn't sink."

She plied her knitting needles as I watched. Her hands were knobbed and rough with hard work like an old woman's, but for all that they moved with an easy skill. "Well, it was not Hammersmith," I said after a long pause. I told her what Adam had said about his right arm.

"You know," she said, "it could have very well been one of the crew."

"Every single one swears he was not anywhere near Ching's cabin that night."

"You can't expect the murderer to come forward and say, 'yes, Captain, I did it,' can you? Have you ever really *looked* at their faces? Not one would make for a choir boy, that's for certain."

"You cannot condemn a man because of his looks."

"That's not what I mean. Heaven knows I'm no portrait myself. But there's a few of them who look downright *savage*. Who knows but one or two might not be running away from the law?"

"Adam told me that hands were not so easy to get these days, now that gold has been discovered in Montana. We were lucky to sign on a full complement."

"Did your husband sign them on?"

"Personally? Not except for Mr. Griggs and Ralston and Cookie. The rest he left to Ralston."

"Hmmmm." Mathilda drew a small scissors from her string bag.

"Adam relies on Mr. Ralston's judgment. He says he is honest, forthright and really quite dedicated to him."

"Hmmmm."

"You do not agree?"

She snipped the yarn with her scissors and tied a different colored thread to her needle. "How much do you know about Mr. Ralston?"

"Why . . . very little. He was married once, rather unhappily." I did not feel I had to divulge the details. "He is close-mouthed. A private person. But that does not mean he would do anything underhanded."

"Hmmmm."

"You are a skeptic," I said smiling. "Don't you believe anyone in this world is good and honest?"

"Of course, I do. You and Roddy, and the captain. Now there's a man I'd trust with my last penny."

"But not Ralston."

"He's too handsome."

I laughed. "Now since when is that a mark against a man?"

"Handsome ones in my experience are conceited. They're blown up with their own importance. Sometimes so much so they feel they can get away with . . ."

"With murder?"

"It's just an expression."

We left it there and began to chat of other things. But Mathilda had planted a seed of suspicion in my mind and that seed grew and grew. Ralston. I had caught a brief glimpse of what lay behind his stiff, arrogant mask. Passion, determination. Had there been a hint of violence, also? "There are a good many things I covet." And Adam had told him from the very start about the Celestial Buddha.

Mathilda's hand on my arm jerked me out of my thoughts. Her eyes rolled toward the door, but she kept chatting away as she laid her knitting aside. Then quickly, with an agility and swiftness which startled me, she stepped to the door flinging it wide.

Jonathan Ralston stood there, his eyebrows raised in surprise.

CHAPTER THIRTEEN

It is not every man caught listening at a door who can collect himself as quickly as Ralston managed to do. "I was just about to knock," he said coolly.

I asked, "What can I do for you, Mr. Ralston?"

"I wondered if you could lend me a needle and thread. One of the buttons on my jacket is loose."

"If you leave the jacket here," I offered, "I would be more than happy to sew it on for you."

"Thank you, but that will not be necessary. I am used to doing for myself." His lips tightened in what I supposed was meant to be a smile.

Mathilda spoke up. "It will hardly be any bother. I have my mending things right here. Come along, slip it off."

He came into the cabin, rather stiff leggedly, and removed his jacket, giving it to Mathilda. She rummaged about in her string bag, brought out several spools of thread and, selecting a dark color, she broke off a length and threaded her needle.

"Which button is it?" she asked, running her finger down the front of the jacket.

He pointed to the bottom one and then stood silently watching her sew, his dark eyes expressionless. If he felt awkward or ill at ease he did not show it.

It was I, for some curious reason, who felt embarrassed and uncomfortable. I asked, "Mr. Ralston, do we have any men in trouble with the law on board ship?" It was the first thing which leaped into my head, and he must have thought the question odd, coming as it did so suddenly without any relevance to jackets or buttons.

"Not that I am aware of, Mrs. Hayworth. Sailors are a rough lot in general. I daresay some of them may have had a few brushes with the authorities."

"They are not a happy lot," I said.

"They are superstitious, that is all. But so is every crew."

"They have cause. Now especially since Ching's been murdered," I pointed out.

"The ghost? But you forget that both Ching and his father's ashes were buried at sea."

Mathilda bit off her thread. "You do not believe in ghosts?" she asked.

"I do not," he answered.

"I thought all sailors had at least a few odd superstitions." She smiled at him.

"I suppose I might have one or two, but they do not include ghosts."

Mathilda held up the coat and shook it. "They say a murder is very bad luck on a ship."

"It is bad luck anywhere. Especially for the murdered man."

Mathilda re-threaded her needle and began to sew at another button. "Now take the legend of *The Flying Dutchman*," she said. "That ship is supposed to have been doomed to sail the seas forever because of a murder on board."

Mr. Ralston curled his lip. "*The Flying Dutchman*. You would be amazed at how many versions there are of that hoary tale. One of the more popular ones is that the ship was manned by an arrogant captain who blasphemed the Almighty and so was condemned by Him to sail for eternity around the Cape of Good Hope."

"Have you ever seen the *Dutchman*?" Mathilda inquired.

"No and I doubt anyone else really has. It is curious, but reports of the *Dutchman* through the years have varied, tallying with each period appropriate to itself; barques, clippers, iron-clads, and the last, I believe, one of those new steamships."

"But if so many have reported seeing her . . ."

"The Cape, Mrs. Jackson, is a stormy and very fearful area. It also shares certain physical properties with the Sahara in that it is ideal for mirages. And just as a thirsty man in the desert can see the waving palms of an oasis, the seaman, alone, buffeted by wind and storm can see the sails of a sister ship that is not there."

Mathilda, finished with her sewing, gave Mr. Ralston his coat. "Thank you, Mrs. Jackson," he said. And to both of us, "Good day."

"Well," said Mathilda, letting out her breath. "I don't believe anything could rattle *him*."

"Do you think he was listening at the door?" I asked in a low voice.

"I'm sure he was. The needle and thread was just an excuse. The button was loose, yes—a quick, lucky thought on his part."

"Why should he be listening?"

"I don't know, except I'd say it's the act of a guilty man."

"I would not call a man guilty of any crime, simply because he had his ear to the door. And, Mathilda, he may have been telling the truth, you know, about the button, I mean."

"Did you see his face when I opened the door?"

"Yes, but I think I would look surprised, too, if I was about to knock and somebody suddenly jerked open the door."

"Well, why don't you ask him, then?"

"Ask him what?"

"If he was listening."

"I'd just as soon ask him if he killed Sam Ching and stole the Buddha."

"It isn't a bad idea," she nodded in reply.

I did not ask him, of course. But I had a conversation with Mr. Phipps the next day, and what he said set my mind wondering about Mr. Ralston all over again. Roxanne and I were taking a turn on deck before going into the saloon for dinner when he came up to us, hat in hand. "Pardon me, Mrs. Hayworth," he said. "But I was meaning to come to you long 'afore this and apologize."

"Apologize?" I asked a little confused. "For what?"

"For letting you find your way back to the cabin after you tended Johnnie. If I had stayed and gone with you . . ."

"It was not your fault," I said. "It was clumsy of me."

"Somebody careless left the hatch open, then must have closed it without knowing you was down there, and I feel responsible."

"Please don't. It is all in the past. And fortunately I came out of it with only a few scratches." I saw no point to telling Mr. Phipps that in actuality it had been the most miserable, horrible half hour I had ever spent in my life.

"I don't think any of us is likely to forget the dressing down Mr. Ralston gave us that night. A hard man, but fair, allus fair."

"You have sailed with Mr. Ralston before?"

"No, ma'am. Never sailed with him. But I know'd him in the past from a place called Rainbow Creek."

There it was again! *Rainbow Creek*. Like the proverbial bad penny turning up when least expected. "What were you doing in Rainbow Creek, Mr. Phipps? From what I understand it is quite some distance from the sea."

"That it is. I'd gone up to try my hand at panning for gold. Thought I'd make a fortune and buy me a tavern. But there were thousands of fools like myself 'afore me, and those never got much either from what I understand. Had to sell my mule to get enough grub to carry me back to the city."

"And Mr. Ralston was there for gold too?"

"I believe so. I never really know'd him except in passing. He's not the kind of man you get close to, if you catch my meaning. He didn't mingle much with the rest of the miners, being a gentleman and foreign born as it were."

"How long was he there?"

"I don't rightly know," he said, twisting his cap.

I sensed he was anxious to be off, but I could not help asking, "When you were at Rainbow Creek, did you know Ah Ching?"

"The Chinaman that was killed?"

"No, his father."

He pulled at his nose. "There was a few Chinamen there. Some come in after we give up the panning. Somehow they allus found a few nuggets where we couldn't. And there was them had a grocery, but . . . no . . ." He shook his head. "To tell you the truth I don't recall any of their names."

"Did you ever hear talk of the Celestial Buddha up there?"

He grinned. "Ma'am, beggin' your pardon, but I don't believe there ever *was* such a thing. There allus was them tales about the Chinamen having big stores of gold and such. But if you could've seen the way they lived. Poor—in shanties tacked up willy-nilly, all crowded together, nothing but raggedy clothes even in the bitter cold of winter. None of the rest of us had much, me leastwise, but we lived a damn sight better."

"Mr. Ching was reputed to have eventually found gold."

"Maybe. But my guess is he never got it in Rainbow Creek."

We exchanged a few more words—I can't remember what because my mind had stuck on Rainbow Creek. Jonathan Ralston had been there, yet he had never said a word about it. I wondered if Adam knew. I burned to ask him, but I dared not. It was clear he resented my speculating on the murder, asking questions, probing and prying into something he felt was none of my business. I thought it terribly unfair since he had a close friend, Ralston, who was privy to everything that happened, and I was forbidden to speak. So it was with this sense of injustice that I soothed my prickly conscience for having broken my promise to Adam and for taking Mathilda into my confidence.

I told her what I had learned from Phipps, and she said she was not altogether surprised. I, in an odd turnabout, found myself again defending Ralston. "He has been roaming the world for some twenty years," I said. "I am sure he does not remember every place he has been."

"He must have a poorer memory than I would give a man of his intelligence credit for," she said. "With Rainbow Creek on so many tongues. And him not saying a word when Bella spoke of it at the table."

After luncheon I was sitting alone in the cabin (Roxanne had remained on deck with Mathilda), still thinking of Ralston, when I saw him go past the porthole window. I waited a minute, then on impulse I went out. Ralston's cabin was catty corner from ours. I stepped across and tried the door. It was unlocked, and looking quickly up and down I darted in.

The place was as small as the passengers', but furnished a little differently, with chronometers on the walls and a bookcase above the writing desk. Apparently Mr. Ralston had been reading one of the books. It lay on the desk with a marker protruding. Curious, I went over to see what it was. *Great Chinese Art Through the Ages.* I opened the volume where the marker had been placed, and found myself looking down at a colored reproduction of a Buddha. A golden Buddha, the eyes of green jade, the garments studded with rubies and diamonds. "The Celestial Buddha," the caption underneath read. "A Ming dynasty work of art, a rare and beautiful object . . . priceless for its religious significance, but in monetary terms the jewels alone would fetch half a million dollars. Stolen some years ago. . . ."

I closed the book quickly as if the pages had suddenly taken flame.

Why not Ralston? I asked myself. But could I condemn a man because he was reading a book on Chinese art? Yet Ralston had been at Rainbow Creek, he knew Ching had the Buddha before any of us, except Adam, did, he was tall. And he had a very strong right arm.

All afternoon I struggled between doubt and certainty as to Ralston's innocence or guilt. By dinnertime I had almost convinced myself that Ralston, indeed, had committed murder and theft when Adam made an announcement at the table which proved my suspicions completely wrong.

"The guilty party has been found," he said flatly, his eyes going round to each of us.

There was a flurry of questions as everyone began to talk at once. Adam put up his hand for silence. "I will tell you who and why and what if you give me the chance."

The man was a seaman, Rogers by name. He had been caught in the act of stealing Mr. Phipps' fob watch, and had, under grueling questioning confessed to the killing. He had heard there was gold in Sam Ching's trunk. Knocking Cookie unconscious, he had gained admittance to Ching's cabin, had killed him and taken the Celestial Buddha. Then in a panic because he was afraid he had been seen (Adam did not mention my name), he had thrown the idol overboard.

To me the news was like the sudden, unexpected, longed for dawning after an endless night. Everyone else seemed as vastly relieved as I. Adam had the steward bring up an extra bottle of wine, and for the first time since coming aboard the *Duchess* I had a truly enjoyable meal. The fact that we were but three days from Shanghai made us all the merrier.

"You will have to meet Roddy," Mathilda said to me. "Better yet, why don't you spend the afternoon with us? Roddy is well acquainted with the city, knows all the shops and bazaars, so he's written. A good shopping tour is what we both need and deserve."

"Why," I said, "that sounds wonderful. I am sure Adam will not mind."

Adam smiled over at us. "I don't see why I should."

"Good," said Mathilda. "It's all settled then."

"Yes," I said. "In three days, if all goes well. And I can't imagine how anything could possible go wrong."

But everything went wrong. Everything.

CHAPTER FOURTEEN

The convivial mood among us lasted all the next day until we were again gathered in the saloon for dinner. I should have known by then that a truce between Hammersmith and Bella Kincaid could never be more than temporary. Perhaps none of it would have happened had Adam been there or had Bella not come to the table well along in her cups, a fact in itself which was enough to raise the missionary's hackles. Where she had gotten the liquor, I do not know, but it was obvious that she had from the high color in her face and the bright snap to her eyes.

The conversation centered on Rogers, Bella maintaining that it was he who had tried to steal her pearls.

"I thought you decided you misplaced them," Mr. Hammersmith reminded her.

"Not the pearls," she said. "I never misplace anything of value."

Mr. Hammersmith helped himself to the potatoes. "I don't remember that man Rogers ever attending one of my Sunday services."

"I wouldn't hold *that* against him," said Bella and then burst out into loud hearty laughter.

Hammersmith watched her, his lips moving soundlessly. "You," he said, pointing his fork at her, "you are beyond the pale."

"Here we go again," said Bella, throwing up her hands. "Another of the preacher's sermons on hellfire and the Devil."

"You would do well to listen, my good woman. Else you will one day pay for your wickedness."

"What wickedness?" Her face turned a shade redder. "Why, do you think I'm the only one at this table who's been wicked?"

There was a short, disquieting silence. Mr. Ralston, who had been present at the table and wordless until then, pushed back his chair, as he always did when words began to fly, and said, "If you will excuse me?"

His departure was like a signal for the storm to break. "Look to your wife," said Bella, thrusting her face across the table at Hammersmith. "Is she redeemed?"

"She is," said Thomas.

"She is, like hell," said Bella.

Edith came to sudden life, springing to her feet. Her eyes were slitted with rage. "Watch your tongue, Mrs. Kincaid."

"I've watched it long enough. And I'm not afraid of you anymore. Why don't you tell him, Edith—huh?"

I tried to interrupt. "Let's not quarrel, please . . ." But my words were like chaff in a strong wind. Nobody seemed to hear them.

Bella kept right on taunting Edith, "Why don't you tell him? Tell the preacher."

Hammersmith said, "She has nothing to tell me. But, you, Bella Kincaid, a scarlet woman . . ."

"She's a whore!" screamed Bella.

I lifted Roxanne from her chair with a view to hustling her out of the saloon before her tender ears should hear more. I had hardly gotten to my own feet when Edith grabbed a knife and lunged across the table at Bella, upsetting a pot of tea. Thomas Hammersmith grabbed his wife's arm, but she had already drawn a thin line of blood, now welling from a cut on the side of Bella's face. I did not think it was more than a scratch, but Bella roared and screamed as if she had been mortally wounded.

Mathilda Jackson tried to dab at Bella's face with a handkerchief, but Bella would not remain still. Edith began to sob. Mr. Hammersmith was shouting. And I stood at the door with Roxanne, indecisive as to whether my duty was to stay to prevent further bloodshed, or whether I should remove Roxanne from the scene as quickly as possible.

It was thus Adam found us. "What is going on?" he demanded. "The commotion can be heard all over the ship."

Everyone began to talk at once.

"Silence!" he roared.

The ensuing hush was like the abrupt cessation of a whistling gale—echoing still with the shriek of voices.

"First off, Charlotte," Adam said. "Get Roxanne to the cabin."

I removed myself without any argument. It had been a distasteful, sickening scene, and I was well out of it. Yet I was curious as to how Adam would resolve the situation.

Mathilda satisfied that curiosity a half hour later when she came to the cabin to give me full details of what had transpired. After my departure, since neither Edith nor Bella were very lucid, and Thomas Hammersmith quite bewildered, it fell to Mathilda to explain the situation. "I was mighty careful not to take sides," she said. "Of course it was easy, since I didn't know what Bella had called Edith was fact."

"Did Edith deny it?" I asked.

"She tried, but Bella wasn't having it. She came right out and said she ran a house in Rainbow Creek and that Edith was one of her girls."

"I can't help but feel sorry for Edith and Thomas too," I said. "It must have shattered him."

"Only for half a minute. I must give credit where credit is due. Once the shock was past he pulled himself together and put his arm around Edith and said, 'She is my Magdalene. Who will cast the first stone?'

"'Damn the first stone,' Bella broke in. 'That woman tried to kill me!' And Edith said, 'She provoked me.' And Bella yelled, 'She cut me. She cut my face. But that ain't all. That woman has threatened to kill me before this . . . yes . . . I got a witness to prove it, Captain, your wife.'

"'Is this true?' the captain asked Edith.

"Edith gave her husband one of those little-girl looks, 'It was only words. I didn't mean it.'

"'Like hell you didn't,' Bella shouted. 'You pulled out a knife *then*—the knife your Papa gave you, you said, and by golly you meant every word.'

"'Perhaps,' said the captain, 'if Mrs. Hammersmith apologizes . . .'

"'I don't want her apology.'

"'What would you have me do, Mrs. Kincaid?' asked the captain. I could tell he was sick of the whole mess. 'Put her in chains, lock her up like Mr. Griggs and Rogers?'

"'Yes,' said Bella. 'I got the law on my side.'

"'I am the law here until we reach Shanghai,' the captain replied. 'Look here, Mrs. Kincaid, I don't like sailing into port with everyone thinking the *Duchess* is a prison ship. Can't we settle this amicably?'

"'No,' Bella was stubborn. 'Furthermore I don't believe that poor sailor, Rogers, ever did kill the Chinaman. It was her.' She pointed to Edith.

"Edith's mouth fell open. 'Well, I'll be a . . .' And her husband said, 'Now if that isn't . . .'

"'You've got murder in your heart,' Bella rolled right over

them. 'And you've seen the Buddha. We were all there at the table when you described it . . . bug-eyed. I wouldn't be surprised if you got it now, hidden under a stack of Bibles.'

"Right then, the captain must have lost any patience he had left. He said he didn't want to hear another word. 'Go to your cabins,' he told them, 'and stay there until we reach port.'"

I sighed, a ragged, heavy sigh. "How we ever managed to get so many quarrelsome and bloodthirsty people together I cannot imagine."

"There's not more than usual, I would say. It's just that we're on this ship, a tight, little island, all marooned by ourselves. Sometimes that'll bring out the best in people, most often it shows up their nuttiness and meanness."

Nuttiness and meanness. We certainly had our share of that aboard the *Duchess*. "Apparently Bella does not believe in Roger's confession," I said.

"Truthfully, I don't hold with all of it myself," said Mathilda. "I can't see anyone, no matter how scared, throwing a fortune overboard, especially when he's killed for it."

"You think Rogers did it, that the Buddha is still somewhere on the *Duchess*?"

"Wouldn't surprise me."

"A lot of good it will do him, then," I said. "When we reach Shanghai, Adam will send Rogers back to San Francisco to stand trial, and he will be hanged."

"For killing a Chinaman?" she said.

"He was a man, and it was murder."

"My dear, I don't know what the law is in England, but in California there is no real punishment except for those who do wrong against a white man."

"Still," I said. "I do not feel Rogers will go free. Nor do I think the Buddha is here. It would have been found by now. The ship, Adam says, has been thoroughly searched, even the cargo moved. I would like to think, I *do* think, the Buddha is at the bottom of the sea. That's where it belongs."

Mathilda shrugged. "You're probably right."

The moment Mathilda left, however, I began to wonder how right I really was—and the old doubts which I thought had been laid to rest with Rogers' confession came back like a swarm of bees. Supposing Rogers had tucked the Buddha away in some cranny, under a board, beneath a row of pipes with an eye to retrieving it some day after the fuss was over? The thought that the fat, smiling Buddha, a symbol now to me of all our ill luck, was still riding with us, gave me a sick sensation.

It was a bad thought, an unreasonable thought. Rogers would have never confessed to murder if he had successfully concealed the Buddha instead of tossing it overboard. He was under lock and key; the accursed idol forever gone. Then why did my nerves jangle so, why did I start at every unexpected sound, dread the coming of night?

I sat reading the usual book, in the usual chair. It was a warm night, and I had left the porthole that gave out into the alleyway open on its hinge. The hour was late, and except for an occasional footfall on the poop deck overhead and the hollow flutter of a sail in the wind, a hushed silence lay over the ship. I read on, my eyes skimming over the words, my mind far from their meaning. I was waiting, listening, I did not know for what.

The tapping came at the opened porthole just as I turned a page. My heart froze to stone, but I did not lift my eyes. I would not look, I must not. If I pretended I had not heard, pretended it was not there, it would go away. The tapping again, insistent, impatient. I lifted my eyes.

The fingers, splayed, like fat yellow slugs were creeping round the window's edge. One following the other, unfolding silently, they fixed themselves in a hold on the glass. The room seemed to darken and grow cold. My arms and legs were encased in ice, my heart frozen. I was not really seeing that thing at the window. How could I? We had left Ah Ching's ashes miles and miles away. I had fallen asleep. I was dreaming, a horrible, horrible dream.

The hand began to crawl slowly down the inside of the glass, and my numbed brain visualized it making its cautious, deliberate way down the length of the door, a hand without a body, humping itself across the floor directly toward me. Clutching, grasping at my skirt, greedily clinging to it . . .

In her bunk, Roxanne suddenly stirred, mumbling aloud. The sound of her voice cut through my paralyzed terror, bringing the hot blood to my face. How dare that . . . that *thing* come into our cabin, how dare it? I snapped the book shut and flung it in frightened rage clear across the room, striking the door. The hand paused (and I had the eerie, sick sensation it was actually *thinking*), then abruptly withdrew. I got to my feet, trembling all over.

After a bit I plucked up the courage to open the door. I

did not know what I expected to find, a hand scuttling along the floor, or climbing the walls, but there was nothing, no one there, only a whispering stillness, the quiet of a ship asleep in the somnolent night. I hesitated a moment and then went down to Mathilda's cabin and rapped softly. There was no answer. She like the others was deep in sleep, and it was selfish of me to disturb her. I was turning away when I heard a sound beyond the door, and the next moment Mathilda, in nightdress and looking a little bewildered, opened it.

"I am sorry," I apologized, "but did you hear anything go past a few minutes ago?" It was not a particularly bright question to ask in view of the silence with which the gloved hand had moved, but it was the only one I could think of.

Mathilda stared at me, not comprehending.

I whispered, "That yellow hand . . . the glove . . . I saw it again."

"Oh, no. One moment, my dear. I'll get into a robe and be with you."

When she joined me, the sash to her robe tied crookedly in her haste, I explained in a low voice how the ghost had reappeared.

"You were wide awake?" she asked.

"Yes, very much so. I was sitting in that chair, reading, when it tapped."

"I wonder," she said, more to herself than to me, "if anyone else saw it."

"If they did we would have heard by now."

"It puzzles me," said Mathilda, "why I've never seen that hand."

"I don't know. But the crew has. There was Billy and Mr. Griggs and Cookie . . ."

"But none of the passengers."

"Yes, that's true enough. But why should it choose our cabin?"

"Perhaps something happened here in the past," Mathilda suggested.

"To Ah Ching? If he were going to haunt any place I should think it would be where he was murdered."

"That seems what they generally do. Maybe he is following his ashes across to see they get a proper burial."

I gave her a sharp look. "You are not laughing at me?"

"My dear, you forget I've got my own ghost story. I'd be the last one to laugh at somebody else's."

"You know," I said, after a silence, "there is something to what you said about Ah Ching anxious to have his remains buried in China. And I think it explains why he comes to this cabin. *If* . . . it is really a ghost."

She lifted her brows.

"Well," I said, "Adam had promised Sam Ching he would carry his father's ashes to their destination no matter what. And . . . well, you know, they went into the sea."

"And Ching is angry."

"It sounds silly, but . . ." I shuddered at the memory of the squat, heavy fingers. ". . . it frightens me."

Mathilda touched my arm. "Charlotte, can't I do something to help? I hate to see you this way. If you feel so scared, why don't we exchange cabins? We've got only tonight and another before we get to port. And as you well know, ghosts don't bother me."

"Roxanne and I might do that," I said slowly. I was tempted, badly tempted to accept her offer. But it was not very practical. I shook my head. "I am afraid Adam would not hear of it. I will just have to keep my window closed and the curtains pulled and somehow bear it out."

"That's the spirit!" said Mathilda. "But if you should change your mind . . ."

"No," I said firmly. "I know I shan't sleep a wink, but I cannot change my mind."

I did sleep, though, in spite of myself. But along about three in the morning I was awakened by the sound of a shot and running footsteps above me. I heard Adam shouting. I pulled on my dressing gown and looked into the passage. Thomas Hammersmith had apparently been aroused too, for I saw him in trousers, his shirttails flying, hurrying on to the deck. Bella's door opened. "What's the fuss?"

"I don't know," I said. Her head disappeared, and a moment later she came out wearing her flounced dressing gown.

Drawn by a feeling of dread—I was sure some terrible calamity had befallen Adam—I locked the door and caught up with Bella.

Adam and Mr. Ralston were standing with a group of seamen a short distance from the poop ladder. When we got closer I saw Mr. Phipps supporting a sailor whose face in the binnacle light was a gray-white. From the murmuring around me I gathered the seaman was none other than Rogers, the confessed thief and killer.

Mathilda edged up to me. "What's happened?" she whispered.

"I don't know yet," I answered.

Adam spoke. "There's no need for you people to be here.

Back to your business. All of you." He was using those measured, controlled tones which meant he was very angry. "Passengers too," he commanded.

They left one by one, reluctantly it seemed, all except Mr. Phipps, Mr. Ralston, Rogers and myself. "Well, Charlotte," Adam said.

I wanted to stay, I wanted to hear, and so I still hesitated.

"Charlotte," Adam said sternly.

I turned and left, but instead of going into the alleyway, I did a sly, unforgivable thing. I hid in the shadow of the ladder.

"How did you get out?" Adam asked.

"I was forced out," Rogers voice came to me, uncertain and shaky. "Someone woke me, and when I opened my eyes there was a gun at my throat.'

"Who was it?"

"I couldn't see. He was dressed in oilskins with a sou'wester pulled down over his nose. He had a low, growly voice. He said if I showed him where I put the Buddha he would hide me and see that I got off the ship without anyone being the wiser. I told him I had thrown it overboard. And he said, 'I don't believe you. Tell me where it is or I'll put a bullet in you now. It'll save you a hanging.'

"So I said, 'All right.' I thought to myself if I led him up to the poop where you was, Captain, he wouldn't dare shoot. So we went out the storeroom, him right behind me with that pistol poking my back. We was halfway across deck when I heard him stumble behind me. I turned real quick and tried to get at the gun. It went off and a bullet whistled past me, singeing my ear. Didn't get me, but knocked me clean off my feet."

"You didn't get a better look at him?" Adam asked.

"No, he ran off before I could come to my senses."

I heard Adam swear under his breath. "All right," he said aloud. "Mr. Phipps, take Rogers back and lock him up."

I heard them move away and then Adam said, "The lad's a bungler from the word go."

"He never killed Sam Ching, did he?" said Mr. Ralston.

"No," said Adam. "He didn't."

CHAPTER FIFTEEN

They were moving toward the stairs, and I dared not stay any longer. I edged round to the entrance of the alleyway and quietly regained my cabin, resisting the impulse to knock on Mathilda's door.

I got into bed and pulled the covers up to my chin, for though the night was warm I found myself shivering. There was something very queer going on, something I was not supposed to know. If Rogers had not killed Sam Ching then why had he confessed? Why was he kept in confinement? Perhaps he had stolen the Buddha after the murderer had been frightened off by my unexpected appearance. But it still did not explain his confession; one does not admit to a capital crime when one is guilty of a lesser one. And now that I reflected on it, it seemed strange that Adam, when he first suspected Rogers, had not taken me to him, hoping I could identify him. Tonight was the first time I remembered seeing the sailor.

"The man's a bungler," Adam had said. Why? What had Roger bungled?

Was it the real murderer who had forced Rogers at gunpoint from the storeroom? Or someone else, someone who, while believing Rogers had killed Ching, thought the Buddha still aboard ship? It seemed incredible to me that the whole sickening business still remained a mystery.

The gray morning light was at the porthole when I finally fell asleep, and it seemed I had hardly shut my eyes when Roxanne was shaking my arm, saying she was hungry. I got dressed feeling as if I had not put my head to a pillow for a week.

Mathilda was the sole occupant of the dining saloon. She looked refreshed and rested, although her night, too, had been broken. "I thought you'd sleep late this morning," she said.

"Not with Roxanne." I longed to tell her what I had overheard, but was too ashamed of having eavesdropped, and on my own husband. Nevertheless, I tried to get her opinion by sounding her out in a roundabout way. "What do you think of Rogers trying to escape last night?"

"Well, he didn't get very far, did he?"

We drank our tea in silence. "Do you think he really killed Sam Ching?" I asked.

"He confessed to it. Although that don't necessarily mean he did it."

"I don't understand."

"You'd be surprised at the people who confess to things they never did. Seems like some has a quirk to their character; either they're braggarts or they got some guilt gnawing at their souls. Puts me in mind of a murder one winter we had in Virginia City. It was the saloonkeeper, a horrible man, watered his whiskey, cheated at cards, beat his wife, ugly as sin. They found him one morning lying across the bar, his eyes fairly falling out of his head. He'd been poisoned, everyone said, by the rot gut he'd been selling to the miners. But the doctor announced it was rat poison, arsenic, and claimed the man was murdered. It was past belief, Charlotte, but five men stepped forward and said they'd done it, proud of it, too, because they had rid the world of such a rotten egg."

"Did they ever find out who really poisoned him?"

"His wife."

I smiled. "So the moral is that Rogers might have made a false confession. Then if he did not kill Ching, who did?"

"A man in oilskins, just as you said from the first." She turned to me. "Did he look like Rogers?"

"It wasn't Rogers." I felt I could tell her that much. "I cannot say how I know, but it was not Rogers."

"If you think back . . ."

"I have thought and thought," I said, picturing the lamplight, recalling the oilskin figure plunging a knife into the man on the bunk. Ching had not cried out. Was he sleeping or too terrified to utter a sound? "But why was he lying on his bunk?" I asked aloud.

"What?" Mathilda asked.

"Don't you see? Ching was expecting Cookie to come to his cabin as he did every night. Ching opened the door for him. He must have. Then he went back to the bunk. He knew the man, oilskins or not, unless the murderer overpowered him before he could make a noise."

Mathilda, her brow furrowed, thought it over. "But then Ching would never have let a stranger into the cabin."

"If that stranger spoke Chinese though . . ."

Mathilda shook her head. "Chinese isn't a language that's

handy to most. I can't think of anyone aboard ship who might speak it, except Cookie."

We looked at one another, and I saw a light dawning in her eyes, very much like the one I felt dawning in mine. "Cookie!" we both said at once.

"Why, of course," I went on. "It all seems so plain now. He knew of the Buddha, he knew the Chings. He has a whole armory of knives. Sam trusted him. And it was too much of a temptation . . ."

"All well and good," Mathilda interrupted, in a calm, practical voice. "But if you remember he was knocked senseless."

"Yes." My face fell. "That is true."

"On the other hand he could have very well murdered Ching, knocked you out, stolen the Buddha, hidden it, removed the oilskins (which he cleverly hid later in Bella's hat box), then given himself a clout. After all, what is a knock on the head when there's a fortune to gain?"

"Mathilda," I said, hugging her. "I think you have solved the mystery."

"You know," she said modestly, "it's only supposing."

"But it makes sense. The most sense of anything yet."

I wanted to tell Adam. How to do it without admitting I had overheard his conversation with Ralston stumped me. But then I decided to edge into the subject sideways, as it were, in the same manner I had done with Mathilda. "Adam," I said, when he had come into the cabin for a handful of fresh cigars, "I have been thinking . . ."

"Oh?" he said absently, opening the lid of the humidor.

"Well, I do think now and then," I said with a forced smile. "And what I thought was that if Rogers did not kill Sam Ching . . ."

"How do you know that?" he asked, throwing me a keen, piercing look.

I pretended to ignore it. "I am just supposing, Adam. Well then, supposing Rogers did not kill Sam Ching, supposing it was Cookie."

"Cookie?" he said in astonishment.

I repeated my reasons for thinking so.

"That is poor logic, to say the least," he said, putting the cigars in his pocket. "I can see Cookie sticking a knife into a man because he spoiled his stew or interfered in his galley. But killing a countryman? No."

"Why not? Why shouldn't he be as avaricious as the next man?"

"Because I have known Cookie for a long time. He is a

happy man, the happiest, I would say, aboard ship, happy to do what he is supposed to do. Cook."

"But even a happy man . . ."

"Not Cookie. Even supposing. Why, can you imagine Cookie knifing his cousin? If he wanted that Buddha so badly he could have simply poisoned him, stolen the idol, and no one would have been the wiser until the corpse began to stink."

I sat down at the dressing table, and combed a stray hair into place before the mirror. "It was Rogers, anyway," I said, watching Adam's face.

"Charlotte, if you don't mind, I would prefer not to discuss the matter any further. I am rather tired of it."

"Did Rogers ever say how he managed to get into Ching's cabin?"

"Must we go on?" Adam said wearily. "Rogers did it. Rogers confessed."

It was a lie, an outrageous lie. "I heard you tell Mr. Ralston . . ." It was out before I could catch myself.

"I see," he said coldly. "That was what the supposing game was all about. You've been eavesdropping again."

"I could not help but overhear."

"Could not help?"

I lowered my eyes.

"Have you told anyone?"

"Mathilda," I said weakly.

He came over to where I was sitting and looked down at me. "You and she had a friendly chit-chat about Rogers' innocence?"

"Well . . . yes . . ."

"Ever since this voyage started," he said, his mouth white with controlled anger, "you have gotten yourself into one predicament after another. I should think that blow on the head would have convinced you to keep your long nose out of this affair."

"My nose is not long," I said, hurt and confused. Why should my talking about Rogers with Mathilda anger him? "And as for being inquisitive, I am no more so than the others."

"I cannot do too much about the others, but you, you are my wife . . ."

"And it is a wife's duty to obey her husband," I said bitterly.

"Edith Hammersmith seems to have no problem in that regard."

"Edith," I said, a red mist rising before my eyes. "Is that how you want me to be? Big eyed, misunderstood, repentant, meek? I am not Edith, and I have no intention of trying to be the least like her."

He opened his mouth to reply when he was interrupted by a knock on the door. It was Mr. Phipps. "Captain, Mr. Ralston would like to see you on the poop, sir," he said. I caught sight of the bosun, his small brown eyes peering at me through the partially opened door. He turned away, embarrassed when he noticed I had seen him. He had probably heard us quarreling. But then, what did it matter? The captain and his wife quarrelling was an old story.

"Thank you, Mr. Phipps, I'll be up directly."

Adam waited a few moments, listening to Phipps' retreating footsteps. Then he said, "Charlotte, I am sorry, but you leave me no alternative. Give me your key."

"What?"

"Give me your key."

"You are not . . ."

"For your own safety, give me your key."

Roxanne was watching us with wide eyes. I gave Adam the key. A moment later, shocked and unbelieving, I heard him turn it in the lock from the outside.

I was a prisoner. Adam had made me a prisoner. The cabin seemed to suddenly shrink in size, the walls coming closer, heavy, oppressive, and a panic rose in my throat, a panic such as I imagined people who are deathly afraid of confined spaces must experience.

Roxanne, tugging at my skirts, brought sense back to my whirling brain. "Is Papa angry?" she asked plaintively.

"Why . . . no . . . no . . ." I stumbled searching for a plausible answer. "He just wants everyone to be out of the way for a while." It was a weak excuse, but, thank God, Roxanne was young enough to accept it without further question.

"Why don't you fetch your dolly and your tea set?" I suggested. "And I will play with you." She went happily into her room.

Together we set out the small china cups and the saucers, the little rose twigged pot, and began our charade of a five o'clock high tea, my mind thinking only of Adam. Had the strain of the storm, the murder, the loss of Billy, Griggs' madness, the near mutiny, been too much for his mind? But he did not appear like a man who had broken down. Harried, tired, anxious, but not insane. His faculties were all there. Then why? Why the key turned in the lock? "For your own safety," he said. Adam was afraid I would speak out of turn, reveal my knowledge that Rogers was innocent. And that fear could only mean one thing.

Adam was protecting the real murderer. But who? Cookie? Or was it Ralston? There was an understanding, a camaraderie, a shared male world of ships and the sea, between Ralston and Adam, a world from which I was excluded. I did not belong in that world. Nor did it seem I was allowed to have one of my own. I was to keep my mouth closed, to sit dutifully, hands folded, obedient behind a locked door, frightened and bewildered and alone, while Adam and Ralston had one another to talk with, exchanging opinions, sharing confidences. Again I seethed with the injustice of it.

And yet, in all fairness, how ridiculous of me to be jealous of their friendship. Envy, bitter envy, had twisted my reasoning. Honestly, I asked myself, would Adam, always scrupulously honest in his dealings, protect a thief and murderer? Perhaps not, that part of me, the sly, demon part which so often got hold of my tongue, said, but that was the Adam you knew on Beacon Street. Not this Adam, the Adam of *The Secret Duchess*. The ship had become his passion; he would sacrifice everything, honor, duty, love for her sake. Adam might suspect Ralston, but he would never say a word. It was not their friendship which mattered as much as Adam's foremost concern—the safety, the success of the *Duchess*. Undermanned, with the second mate in chains, how could he sail his precious ship with no officers?

By late afternoon Roxanne began to get restless as she always did when confined for too long, running from wall to wall, slamming into the chairs, climbing onto the bunk and jumping up and down, like some penned-up animal gone crazy. This was the last day of our voyage and it seemed to be the longest of any I had spent thus far.

"Come and sit for awhile," I said to Roxanne.

"In a moment, Mama. Just one more jump." She leaped from the bed, falling against the wall. I went over to pick her up. She was laughing. "Didn't hurt myself . . . but . . . oh, Mama! . . . look . . . !" She was pointing to the wall behind me.

I turned. A small alcove, a very small one, had appeared in the wall near the floor where there had been none before. But it was not the unexpected opening which set my mouth agape.

From the dark recess there was a faint glitter, and a passing ray of the afternoon's dying sun chose that moment to slide through the porthole, lighting the alcove into a dazzling, fiery sparkle.

I bent closer to have a better look. Green eyes from a golden face looked blankly into mine.

It was the Celestial Buddha.

CHAPTER SIXTEEN

Stunned and speechless I stared at the smiling image, a ruby twinkling here, a diamond there. I saw no beauty in the idol, felt no awe, no reverence, no desire to possess it, only revulsion. So much misery, so much blood spilled, so many lives cursed for this piece of statuary. A fortune lay at my feet, one with which to buy ships and castles and anything my heart fancied, and it filled me with nothing but loathing. Evil, ugly . . .

"Mama . . ." Roxanne brought me out of my trance. "Mama, what is it?"

"It . . ." I bit my lip against the sudden trembling of my jaw. "It . . . it is a doll, a large, foreign doll. It does not belong to us."

"But why is it here?" she asked innocently.

"It . . . it is here for . . . for safekeeping, I suppose." Safekeeping. Secreted, hidden behind the wall. In falling Roxanne must have triggered the mechanism which had opened the alcove. "We must close the panel again, Roxanne. And, darling," I put my finger to my lips, "it is to be our secret. Not one word. No one must know, do you understand?"

She shook her head in assent, her eyes wide with delight. "Not even Papa?"

"Papa." Did Adam know? "Not for now," I said. "We shall tell him later."

I tried to close the panel, my fingers shaking as if stricken with palsy, in terror, now that Adam would arrive at any moment. For some reason, which I did not fully comprehend then, I felt he must be kept ignorant of my discovery. The wall was smooth, satin smooth, nowhere could I find a bump, a button, a ridge. Perspiration beaded my brow as I continued to feel for the exact spot which would move the panel, since it refused to budge by pulling on it. "Roxanne, show Mama how you fell."

She climbed upon the bunk, her eyes merry, excited with our new game. She stood, teetering, bending her knees and at last, with a "Watch me, Mama!" leaped, hitting the wall again.

The panel slowly closed.

I sat down upon the chair, folding my hands tightly, so tightly a knuckle cracked, willing my mind to blankness. It was better that way. Don't think. Don't think. Roxanne chattered on; I nodded and smiled, and nodded and smiled, like a deaf mute, hearing nothing, saying nothing.

I was still sitting there when the steward came with our dinner. If he thought it odd to have been given a key to gain entry and instructed to use it when he left, he said nothing. Shortly afterwards, Mathilda tapped upon the porthole window. "We are having dinner here tonight," I said, going to the door, fearful lest she should try it or ask to come in. Aside from a disinclination to speak to anyone, I think I should have died of shame, if she had discovered I could not open the door.

"You haven't forgotten our excursion tomorrow?" she spoke through the window.

I looked at her blankly.

"We were going to do the bazaars with Roddy, remember?"

"Yes . . . yes, I have not forgotten." Roddy. Shopping in the bazaar. Tomorrow. I wanted to laugh; I wanted to cry. *Tomorrow*. The world had closed down so about my head, I could not visualize a tomorrow.

She went away. In an hour the steward returned for the tray. I had helped Roxanne with her meal, but I had not eaten a morsel myself. The steward made some remark about my untouched plate to which I thought I gave an appropriate reply. But as he reached the door he threw a quizzical, half fearful look over his shoulder. Was he thinking my mind had gone, like Griggs', and the captain, the poor beset captain, must now cope with a daft wife?

I started undressing Roxanne for bed at seven. She was most unwilling, twisting and turning and protesting it was far too early. Our shared secret and the knowledge we would reach Shanghai on the morrow had excited her past fatigue. In her nightdress, finally, she stamped her foot in exasperation. "I shan't go to bed!" she shouted.

My hand shot out, and I cracked her smartly across the cheek. We both stared at one another for the space of five seconds, stunned. I was one to spare the switch, and my striking out at her had been totally unconscious.

Immediately the shock was over she began to shriek in earnest. I was beside myself. Now the steward would say I was not only crazy but murdering my child. I gathered her up in my arms and held her without speaking until her sobs subsided. "Come," I said, "I will read *Aesop's Fables* to you until you fall asleep." The famous fables, along with Grimm's and Trollope were the staples of our shipboard library.

I read the tale of the *Fox and the Grapes,* the donkey, the bear, the crow, and the crow again—she liked that one— and still her eyes remained wide. "Roxanne," I said at last, shutting the book, "we have not said our prayers."

She started to get out of bed. "No . . . stay. I shall kneel beside you. You can say yours from your pillow."

I knelt down and bowed my head. "The Lord is my Shepherd . . ." I began, and her voice murmured after me. I went through that simple prayer aloud, but in my heart there was a far different prayer. Dear God in heaven, please show me a way. Please let there be some reason, some good reason why the Buddha is here. And, I added, please let Adam be unaware of its presence.

I knelt there for a long time, repeating the words of Roxanne's bedtime prayer over and over in a dull monotone, until I realized Roxanne had become silent. Lifting my head, I saw she was sleeping peacefully. Her auburn curls were spread upon the pillow, one white, slender, fragile, defenseless arm thrown out over the coverlet. As I gazed at her I wished fervently I was a child again, with nothing to awaken to but a breakfast of porridge and milk tea and a trip to the bazaars.

I went back into my own cabin and sat heavily upon the bunk, the full weight of my terrible discovery at last dragging me down into the depths of misery. I could not put off thinking about it any longer. The Buddha secreted behind the panel, the Buddha my mind had sought to dismiss, became a palpable reality. It was there. I could not see it, but it was there, smiling in the darkness of the alcove, grinning at me through the wall, grinning in terrible malevolence.

Perhaps, I thought in a sudden upsurge of hope, Adam did not even know of the alcove's existence. But the thought withered, died, a few moments after it was born. Everything, all that he had said, all that he had done, indicated otherwise.

He had supervised the refitting of the ship himself. He knew every twist and turn of her, every niche, every shelf, every cupboard. Was there anyone else who knew the captain's cabin had a secret hiding place? Ralston? But wouldn't he be foolish to conceal it under Adam's nose? No, whichever way I looked at it, turned it around in my mind, I could not escape the fact that Adam, himself, had put the Buddha there.

Had he stolen the Buddha? Ralston's book had said the Buddha was worth a half million dollars, and Adam, deeply in debt, a good part of his valuable cargo spoiled, everything, his entire future, riding upon the success of *The Secret Duchess*'s first voyage, had been tempted, had seen in the dazzling, golden Buddha the end to financial worry. I had been locked in, not for my own safety, but for the Buddha's. Adam was afraid with Shanghai so close it might yet be discovered.

The second question I asked myself—I had to—was far more painful. Had he killed Sam Ching to gain possession of the idol? *No!* Every nerve in my body screamed against it. Robbery, maybe, yes, whatever, but never murder. Not Adam. And yet how well did I know Adam, this man who shared my bed, this man who was the father of my child?

Our courtship was not a long one, but even if it had been, what woman really knows her prospective groom, a suitor who is careful to put his best foot forward? Yet, I reasoned, clinging, grasping at any straw, we had been married for over four years.

Very true, I answered myself, and how much had I seen of Adam during those years? Not very much. He had been at sea—away—for most of the time. I knew that he could be gentle, kind, considerate, loving, a doting father. But had I not seen the other side of him these past weeks? Stubborn, narrow, tyrannical, given to rages, anything but a loving husband.

"No," I said again; I could not, would never believe it, even if he should stand before me and confess he had murdered Ching. Someone else had plunged that knife through the little man. That person, surprised by me, had fled before he had stolen the Buddha. Adam had found me unconscious on the threshold, and seeing that Ching was already dead, the trunk opened, had taken the idol.

But—but, that insidious, small, doubting, horrid part of my mind argued, Sam Ching had unbolted his door because he *knew* the person who knocked. There were only two men on board Ching trusted—Cookie and Adam. Supposing—ah, that supposing again—Adam had come to Ching, not because of the Buddha, but to persuade the little Chinese to dispose of the urn which held his father's ashes, those ashes which were causing so much trouble among his superstitious crew. "Let me give your father a burial at sea," I pictured Adam pleading. And Sam Ching, stolid, adamant, replying, "No." They had argued and Adam, in a fit of temper, killed him.

With Cookie's knife?

But how did I *know*, how did anyone know, it had been Cookie's knife? The weapon had never been found. Adam could have stabbed him with any knife, the very one with which he cut his cigars, for instance.

No! Never! I could not accept that. Stealing the Buddha was one thing, but murder . . .

"Say nothing of what has happened tonight," he had warned me. And his fingers had dug into my shoulder. "How much did you see?" Certainly he had not pushed me into the hold. That I had imagined. But I had not imagined his coldness, his easy anger, his admonishment to "keep my long nose out of the matter." And now he had locked me in the cabin.

Was I wed, bound, "until death did us part," to a man I did not know, a thief, a murderer?

My tortured mind, pulling first one way then the other, made my head throb, a pounding ache which threatened to burst my skull. I thought I would surely commence screaming, run amok, crashing my miserable head against the walls to relieve the pain. If only I did not have to keep it bottled inside. If only . . .

And that is when I began to write it all down.

It has been weeks now since I wrote the above. The end of my story, the most incredible part of it, came long before, but now for the first time I feel able to put it to paper.

I spent the long night writing. It was dawn when I finished. My words staring at me in black and white did nothing to quell the tumult inside me as I had hoped. I was still alone, isolated on an island of misery and doubt. I felt if I did not speak to someone I would surely go over the edge.

Adam never came. I had not expected him to, what with Shanghai so close. When I looked out the porthole in the blood red light of the rising sun, I saw two gulls skimming the waves. We would reach anchorage in a matter of hours. Then what? I knew I could not conceal my knowledge of the Buddha from Adam, nor my suspicions. And I was mortally afraid, terrified of him.

The steward came with our morning tea. Ordinarily a taciturn, reserved man, he was in high excitement. Land had been sighted, the long, interminable voyage of our first port of call was nearly over. And because of his high-strung state he forgot to lock the door after he had deposited the tray.

Roxanne was still asleep. As soon as I guessed the steward was out of the alleyway I stole out and went and tapped softly at Mathilda's door. She opened it, already dressed, a look of mild surprise in her eyes. I put my finger to my lips. Her arm reached out and drew me inside. And then, unable to control myself, I began to blubber and sob like a child.

For a long while she held me in her arms, not saying anything, letting me have my cry. She was closer to me, more dear, than she had ever been. I felt as if she was the real mother I had always wanted, not like my own mother, poor darling, weak, always at a loss, falling apart so easily at every minor crisis, failing me most miserably when I needed her most. When at last my sobbing had subsided, Mathilda sat me in a chair, brought a damp cloth and dried my eyes and tear-stained cheeks, and then waited patiently for me to speak.

"I . . . I . . . oh, Mathilda . . ." I looked at her appealingly, for suddenly I could not find the words, and the whole shame, the horror of Adam's crime descended upon me once more.

"You needn't tell me what's bothering you, if you don't want to," Mathilda said kindly. "A good cry is all you need."

I nodded, the tears beginning to spill again, but the heaviness in my heart remained. "I must tell someone . . . oh, Mathilda . . . I found the Celestial Buddha."

She looked at me in astonishment.

"It is there . . . in the cabin . . . behind a panel . . . and I think . . . I think . . . Adam . . ." I bit my lip and shook my head. "I . . . I have not slept a wink worrying about it. Not knowing what to do. He is my husband . . . I . . . I cannot go against him, and yet . . . What shall I do?"

"Does anyone know?"

"None but Roxanne. Roxanne . . ." I got to my feet, wringing my hands. "I must go . . ."

"Run along, then," said Mathilda. "As soon as I finish packing I'll come down. We'll think of something."

When I got back Roxanne was kneeling on her bunk, her face pressed against the porthole. "Look Mama, we are there. Look!" Peering over her shoulder, I could just make out in the distance a cluster of ships at anchor and several quays with tiny figures like small dolls scurrying to and fro.

"Are we going to the bazaar with Mrs. Jackson?" she asked eagerly.

The bazaar again. "Yes . . . yes. We will speak of it later."

I was helping Roxanne into her dress when I heard the

door to the cabin open and, thinking it was Mathilda, said, "I am in here with Roxanne."

But it was not Mathilda. It was Adam. He came and stood in the doorway of the cubbyhole. I bent my head, avoiding his eyes, and busied myself with the long row of buttons at the back of Roxanne's dress.

"The steward forgot to lock the door," he said, and my heart lurched in my breast. "Damn the fellow."

"Am I going to be a prisoner then, even in port?" I said, turning at last. And before he could answer, "You know that Mrs. Jackson and I had planned to shop. She wants me to meet her husband. Roxanne is so looking forward to it."

"Oh, Papa. Please say yes."

He gave her a weary smile. "I don't see how . . ."

"Oh, Papa, please," Roxanne begged.

"I shall have to think about it." He turned and walked to the table where his cigars were kept and selected one. We were there, both of us, Roxanne and I, at the doorway watching him. I held my breath. His eyes studied me for a few moments. "Very well," he capitulated. "But, Charlotte, you must promise me you will not leave the ship with Mrs. Jackson until everyone else has debarked."

Was he thinking that once everyone was safely gone, including myself, he could remove the Buddha, take it ashore and sell it to some unscrupulous merchant with no questions asked? "I promise," I said.

A few minutes later Mathilda arrived. She was wearing her shawl, carrying her bonnet and her habitual string bag. "I've left instructions to have my baggage taken down as soon as we touch the wharf," she said.

"Adam has made me promise we would not leave until the others are off the ship."

"That won't delay us long. They're all champing at the bit. I've never seen people so eager to get their feet on solid ground." She looked quite happy. And why shouldn't she be? For her the journey was over. She was going to be reunited with her husband, a husband she had been married to for over thirty years. They had gone through many hardships and disappointments together, shoulder to shoulder, sharing everything. *Their* marriage had been a success.

"Now then," Mathilda said cheerfully, "what shall we do about you?"

"There is nothing you *can* do," I said despondently. "It was wrong of me to burden you with my problem."

"You mustn't say that. What are friends for?"

"I suppose my only recourse is to go on and pretend I never saw the wretched idol."

"Did you really see it? Perhaps you may have fallen asleep and your worried mind . . ."

"No, no. I tell you it is here."

I went to the wall and stooping, felt along the polished panels, pressing the place where I remembered the Buddha was hidden. "Roxanne," I explained, "jumped from the bed and fell against the wall . . . here." I pressed and the panel silently slid open. I stepped aside.

Mathilda gasped. "Well, I'll be a . . ." She got down on her knees and carefully lifted the Buddha from the alcove.

"Heavy," she remarked.

She got to her feet and sat down on a chair, the Buddha in her lap. She passed her hands over it, those bony, work-worn hands, caressing the head, her fingers sliding over the rubies and diamonds. And then she looked up at me. Her eyes held a strange, triumphant glitter.

"At last," she said. "At last."

I was too bewildered to speak.

"Thank you, Charlotte. Thank you."

"Why do you thank me?" I said perplexed, thinking surely my ears had deceived me.

"Do you realize how many years I have searched for this?"

"*You?*"

She nodded, her eyes distant and hazy. "Years. Ten I think it is since Roddy and I first saw it."

"But you never said . . ."

"We were going up a mountain trail near Rainbow Creek. We had this old tired jackass, and he was carrying the sum of what we had to show for years of hard work; a few tin pots, an old frying pan, our bed rolls. We stopped to rest beside a stream and I fell asleep. The next thing I knew Roddy was shaking me. 'Shhh . . ,' he pointed.

"And there beyond a screen of trees I saw two Chinamen. One—though I didn't know until much later—was Ah Ching. The other was old, and even with his yellow skin I saw he was very sick. He gave Ah Ching something wrapped in burlap. Ah Ching uncovered it . . . and it was the Celestial Buddha.

"Oh, how it shone and sparkled in the afternoon sun! The pot at the end of the rainbow. We would have stolen it then, but some miners were coming down the trail and Ah Ching and the old man hurried off into the trees. Ever since that day we've been after it . . . and now . . ."

Befuddled with shock, I cried, "But it is not yours!"

"It *is* mine," she said. "I've killed twice for it and I'll do it again, if need be . . ."

"Twice?" My mouth went dry.

"Ah Ching was the first. After losing him and finding him, I don't know how many times, Roddy finally tracked him to San Francisco, but it was me who discovered him in that little shop of his on Powell Street. I thought a knife would be quick and quiet . . ."

A knife. My cheeks were burning hot. I recalled the evening we had first discussed Ah Ching's death at the dinner table and Mathilda saying, ". . . you read about it in the papers . . . one of them is always getting a knife stuck in his back . . ." And then she had calmly buttered a roll.

"He hollered and squealed so," Mathilda was saying, "I had to run for it. Then we heard Sam, his son, was planning to take his pa's ashes to Canton, and the Buddha was going with him. So I sent Roddy on ahead while I kept close watch on the sailings."

She shifted the Buddha in her lap. "I didn't want to kill Sam. I tried every which way to get into that cabin. I could unlock the door with a hairpin, as you remember, but he had it bolted on the inside. In between times I was doing the ghost trick with a glove on a stick and a few bits of wire, hoping you and a superstitious crew would force him out. All I needed was a general hubbub, the door open and a few minutes with the trunk . . ."

The yellow glove, the yellow fingers, tapping at my window, creeping slowly down the side of the life boat.

"It did cause a disruption, but Ching stayed put like a leech. I even tried smoking him out . . ."

The fire, and Mathilda watching Roxanne so obligingly while I went to fetch Adam.

". . . then I hit upon the best plan of all. There were only two people who Sam would unlock the door for, Cookie and your husband. I decided to impersonate Cookie since he came regularly to Ching's cabin."

It could not have been a woman, I told Adam, and he had agreed. "You knocked him unconscious?" I asked, still finding it all hard to believe.

"I'm a strong woman, Charlotte. I've done a man's work all my life, since I was hardly older than kitten here. It was a dark, wet night, and just when Cookie was crossing the deepest shadow, I tapped him on the skull. He didn't as much as say 'boo' when he fell . . . I got into his oilskins and went to Ching's cabin. I had watched Cookie do this from my window many times. So I knew just how many raps to make . . ." She tapped on the wall beside her. "And what to say. I had learned a few words of Chinese myself, so it wasn't hard to imitate. But as soon as Ching let me in I saw I wasn't going to fool him. There was no other way to get the Buddha except to kill him. I came prepared to do that . . . a long kitchen knife. And he didn't even have the chance to open his mouth. I laid him on the bunk. He was a little man, light as a feather. I pried the trunk open, and just as I was reaching for the Buddha I heard him moan. I got to him before he could make another sound and was finishing him off when, by golly, if you didn't appear at the door. I thought if you screamed I was done for, but you didn't, and when you had your back turned to me . . . well, I needn't tell you about *that*.

"I still think I had time to get the Buddha," she reflected, "but seeing you scared me. I thought surely someone would have heard sounds by then, or maybe Cookie had come to, so I lost my nerve and bolted. As it was I couldn't be sure you hadn't recognized me, and then when nothing was said, I figured maybe the knock you got caused a little lapse in your memory. That if you thought about it long enough . . ."

Incredulous, I asked, "You pushed me down the hatch, into the hold?"

"You see, Charlotte, I was into this deep. I couldn't *chance* anything," she explained amiably, rationally, as if the whole crazy, bloody confession was one of her many tales, so like the ones she had entertained me with during our passage. What she was saying was too impossible to be true. All of it. It was fancy, pure fancy on her part. "But I might have been *killed*," I pointed out.

"I guess so."

Shocked to the core, I said, "Killing does not seem to mean anything to you. Have you no feelings?"

"Feelings?" she asked scornfully. "Feelings is for those who've not gone to bed hungry night after night, for those who've not worked like a slavey from the time they was no bigger than a bean shoot, for . . . but why go on? Feelings is a luxury I could never afford."

Calm, serene Mathilda, I had thought, and envied, Mathilda who was above the petty bickering and quarreling, when, in reality, her placidity was a simple lack of any human feeling at all. Clever Mathilda, acting out her role of motherly affection, my friend, my confidante; and how easily, how stupidly I had been deceived. "When I suspected Bella . . ."

"I had to hide the oilskins. I couldn't get rid of them as easy as the knife."

"And the others we talked about, Ralston, the Hammersmiths . . ."

"Well, someone *did* steal it. I knew it wasn't the captain. He wouldn't steal a goose egg, not even if it was the golden one."

I turned my face away, sick with shame. This hard-bitten woman, this creature who could kill without a qualm had more faith in Adam's honesty than I. She had consorted with all types, thieves and liars, and braggarts and murderers. She *knew* people, and she knew a trustworthy man when she saw one. But what did I know? Nothing. What had I seen? Only my poor twisted self and a distorted vision of a man I purported to love.

"They searched the ship," she said, "the captain and Mr. Ralston, something I was itching to do myself. But naturally I couldn't look anywhere except in the passengers' cabins. The captain'd be on to me if he caught me poking around in the fo'castle. Then when he said Rogers had confessed killing Sam Ching and had thrown the Buddha overboard I suspected a trick. On the other hand Rogers might very well have stolen the Buddha and lied about getting rid of it. I was in a quandary. We were getting closer and closer to Shanghai, and there'd be Roddy waiting for me. And I coming empty handed. Another failure. So many failures, all the years getting someplace too soon or too late, just missing the brass ring. I couldn't bear it. So I put on the oilskins and got Rogers out of the storeroom. But when I saw he was heading for the poop deck, it came clear to me I had been right in the first place. It was all a hoax . . ."

She was silent for a few moments. I heard the rumble and rattling of the anchor chain, the hurried footsteps above on the poop. I hoped, I prayed, Adam, Ralston, the steward, anyone would come to the door. But the men were all busy, Adam on the bridge, the passengers, after so long a voyage, eager to go ashore. There would be no one.

Mathilda was speaking again. "It was then that it struck me like a thunderbolt. The captain had found the Buddha and had hidden it for safekeeping."

Safekeeping. The word was like a thorn stuck into my flesh. I had thought of that myself, briefly, for the space of five seconds, then dismissed it. Dismissed it because my fool's head was so certain Adam was a thief.

"I'd already searched the chartroom once," Mathilda continued, "but I searched it again. When I couldn't find it, I guessed it might be here. So I brought out the yellow glove hoping you'd get scared enough to exchange cabins with me. But I needn't have gone to the worry and trouble, since, in the end, you led me right to it." She opened her string bag and carefully lifted the Buddha into it.

"I don't know why you have told me all this . . ." I began, a taste of bitter gall on my tongue.

"Why, I suppose it's because I'd like someone to know that for once in her life Mathilda Jackson accomplished what she set out to do."

"Murder?" I asked scornfully. "You count *that* an accomplishment?"

"What does it matter? Two Chinamen less. There are millions out there."

No feelings, she had said. Feelings were a luxury. "Take it, then," I said in disgust. "Take it and get out. But God will punish you."

"That's exactly what Hammersmith would say." She curled her lip. "And it's rot. I'm not like the good preacher. I don't believe in waiting for my pie in the sky. After a lifetime of grubbing around for bread crusts, I want that pie now."

"You have it," I said. "Go on. What are you waiting for? Get out!"

"Not so fast, Charlotte dear. Get out, you say, and you hollering your head off the minute I step out the door?"

She reached into the string bag and pulled out a gun. I looked at the thing, a long, ugly revolver, and my skin shriveled. "You have what you want," I said, my lips dry as dust. "Why must you kill me?"

"I'm not planning to kill you, Charlotte. You are too valuable to me at the moment alive. You and me and Roxanne are going shopping in the bazaar just as we intended. Your husband knows of our little expedition. He might think it funny if I went down the gangway alone. So put on your bonnet, my dear . . ."

"No!"

"Yes and yes and *yes*." Her eyes blazed. "It won't be you I'll shoot, but that lovely, sweet kitten of yours. Now you wouldn't want that, would you?"

I put on my bonnet. Roxanne was still kneeling on her bunk, her face pressed to the porthole. "Come along, darling," I said with a forced, stiff smile. "We are going ashore."

She looked up at me, her face flushed with excitement. Oh God, I thought, what will happen to us? Would that mad woman be satisfied to disappear into the crowd with the wretched Buddha, or would she and her husband take the two of us and kill us in some dark alley. And Adam would never find us, never know. I clasped Roxanne to me for a few moments, then I put on her bonnet.

"My good one?" she asked happily. "The one with the blue ribbons?"

The one with the blue ribbons. Blue, pale blue.

Yes, she would kill us. It would mean nothing to her, and it would give her and her Roddy time, time to escape.

We went out into the alleyway. "Make one sound, one yip," Mathilda whispered, "and the kitten will get a bullet."

We walked across the deck to the gangway. The ship looked odd, different now that it was deserted. I thought of the hours, the days I had spent on her, hating her, wishing *The Secret Duchess* had never come into my life, never dreaming there would come a time when I would feel reluctant to leave her.

Through a dazed blur of cold terror I saw the wharf as we descended. A mass of people, all colors, all shapes, shouting and milling about. I heard the creaking of winches, smelled the foreign odor of sweet spices. It was like a distant picture seen through clouded glass, and to this day I cannot recall in detail my first view, my first sight of the Orient.

When we reached the wharf my legs, unsteady with fear and accustomed as they were to the pitch of the ship's deck, threatened to double under me. "Keep going," said Mathilda, smiling through clenched teeth, her arm linked in mine. I felt the nudge of the gun, hard and cold, in my side.

The next moment we were engulfed by the crowd. They pressed against us, a tide of human bodies. Roxanne, clinging to my hand, began to whimper as she fought for air. I stooped and picked her up.

"Make way!" Mathilda shouted.

The mob thinned, but only for a moment. They closed in again like a solid wall, and suddenly, to my astonishment, I was looking into the brown eyes of Mr. Phipps, the bosun.

"Get out of my way!" Mathilda ordered.

Phipps only grinned.

Mathilda tried to pull me aside, but the human wall was all around us, to the side, in back, a tight ring; and they were all men from *The Secret Duchess*.

Mathilda, in a fury now, let go me and began to brandish her revolver. "Stand aside or I'll shoot!" she yelled.

A hand darted up from somewhere and got hold of her wrist, twisting it. Another hand caught the gun as it fell.

Then I heard Adam's voice. "Good work, Ralston."

The crowd parted as Adam came through.

CHAPTER SEVENTEEN

Adam stretched his arms out and Roxanne went into them with a happy little cry. He hugged her tightly, kissing each cheek, murmuring, "It is all right. Papa is here. It is all right."

I stood there, so close to those two, and yet so far, like a cold, hungry waif outside a baker's shop window. Ignored. Beyond the pale. The murderer had been caught, the Buddha recovered and we were safe, Roxanne and I. But the thing I now wanted most in the world, the coming together of Adam and me, was as remote as ever. It served me right, I thought bitterly, if I had obeyed Adam, trusted him, had confided in him instead of a stranger, I would not be standing here on the verge of blubbering like a fool. I turned my face away.

"Go along with Ralston," I heard Adam say.

Adam did not want me. He did not even care to look at me. He was dismissing me. It was humiliating, unbearable. I thought of losing myself in the crowd, disappearing; I did not care where I went or what would become of me. Everything is over now, I thought. I shall trudge the streets of this alien Eastern city, threading my way through corrupt, stinking alleys, along avenues of perfumed pagodas, blind to beauty and ugliness alike because it did not matter, nothing mattered. So immersed was I in this self-pitying vision, I jumped with shock when I felt a hand on my arm. "Charlotte!"

Adam turned me about, and we looked into each other's eyes, mine puzzled, his searching. He held my face between his hands, his gaze concerned, warm with tenderness, a gaze I once knew but had lost somewhere in memory. "Charlotte, I had not meant to put you through this." It was the old Adam, my friend, my lover, my husband.

"No . . . no," my voice struggled against the ache in my throat. "It was all my fault. I found the Buddha, you see, and . . . and I thought it was you and I told Mathilda, and . . ."

He kissed me. There in front of the whole of Shanghai,

Adam kissed me. When I lifted my head I saw Ralston watching us. He had Roxanne on his shoulders, and she, child as she was, had forgotten us and was gazing about happily. And then Ralston did something I never thought possible. He smiled. He smiled at Adam and me, a happy, full, beautiful, blessed smile.

It was not until later that night Adam and I had the opportunity to talk. He had been busy all afternoon with the ship's business (the furs were in far better condition than he had first thought): arranging for the transport of Mr. Griggs and Mathilda Jackson to San Francisco, hunting up a Buddhist temple where, to his relief and the monks' astonished gratefulness, he deposited the golden idol. He had also made a request of them, a request which astounded me. He had asked the monks to see to it that Ah Ching's ashes went on to Canton. "You see," Adam said. "A promise is a promise. The urn we buried at sea had nothing in it but sawdust."

We were sitting side by side on the bunk, talking in low tones. Roxanne was asleep in her cubbyhole, exhausted, for Ralston had taken her on a tour of the bazaars as promised, though without me. I had lost my taste for bazaars.

"Mathilda was clever," said Adam. "I never suspected until the last."

"Nor I—but how did you know?"

He smiled and kissed the tip of my nose. "No woman sets out on a shopping tour with a bag so heavy it weights her arm down. The minute I saw her I knew she had the Buddha."

"You must have guessed it was gone."

"Yes, I did, a lucky guess. When I came to the cabin before we docked, I took one look at your face and knew you were upset; and from the way you avoided my eyes, I calculated you were hiding something from me. You always were transparent, Charlotte, not a very good liar. What is it now? I asked myself. I was standing at the table getting a cigar from the humidor when I happened to glance over at the wall, more especially at the panel where the Buddha was hidden (something I did frequently) and there I saw a sticky hand mark . . ."

"Mine," I said. "My hands were perspiring . . ."

"Just so. I thought, she's found it. Shall I confront her and ask her point blank? Meanwhile you and Roxanne were badgering me to allow you to go ashore with Mathilda, and it suddenly occurred to me that, of course, you would tell Mathilda about the Buddha, if you hadn't already done so."

"I did," I said. "And Adam, I am so terribly . . ."

"Yes. Well, I did a terrible thing too. I decided to use you and the Buddha as decoys. I had never seriously considered Mathilda as the murderer, but if she were, I knew she would not leave the *Duchess* without the idol. So before we put down anchor I gathered the few hands I trusted together and told them to mingle with the crowd on the wharf, all the while keeping a sharp eye on the poop deck for a signal from me. The rest you know."

"And Roderick Jackson was never found?"

"No. But I can make a very good guess the moment he saw Mathilda apprehended he melted quickly into the crowd. It is just as well, for I doubt we could have held him for any crime."

We did not speak for a few moments. The warm, breathless night drifted in through the open porthole. There was a distant murmur of voices, and from somewhere far across the dark water a bell clanged.

Adam said, "It has been miserable for you, Charlotte, and miserable for me."

"Hush . . . it is over now."

"Over now, thank God. But when I saw you there, pale as death, lying on the deck of Ching's cabin, I felt as if you had been murdered instead of he and that I had done it."

"No, Adam . . ."

"Somehow I knew from the moment Sam Ching told me of the Celestial Buddha, something terrible would happen. But *you* . . . To live day after day with the knowledge that your life was in danger, and there was the crew muttering and giving me dark looks and the passengers at loggerheads, and Mr. Griggs—I tell you there were times I thought I would go mad as he."

He got up and began to pace from one wall to the other. "I cannot explain how terrified I was. For years it had been my goal to have my own ship, to be its master. I could not wait for the dream to come true. And then—a murder. And you a witness.

"If I could have caught the culprit. But there were no clues except for the kitchen knife which anyone could have stolen, and your vague description of a man in oilskins. Nothing.

"I tried to lure the murderer out of hiding with Rogers, a tough young lad with not the most savory of pasts, but dependable on the whole and willing to go through the whole farce, confession and all. I armed him—I could do no less—and warned him to be alert since I had the feeling the murderer and thief were one, and that whoever it was would be after him. And I was right, except that poor Rogers, after several wakeful nights, fell sound asleep on the very one that mattered. Afterwards he was terribly ashamed and sheepish and I imagine would have felt even more so had he known his assailant was a woman.

"Nevertheless, our killer had slipped through the net, and we were getting closer and closer to Shanghai. And I was more than ever worried about you. You would not stay put. You kept going on and on, asking questions, speculating as to who the guilty party was. I simply had to be stern and lock you in the cabin."

"But why didn't you tell me?" I asked. "Tell me everything?"

"How could I? It was bad enough as it was. How could I burden you further? Tell you the Buddha, that accursed Buddha, was in our cabin? And nowhere else I could safely hide it?"

"But I am your wife."

"Just so." He kissed me. "And my love and more dear to me than anything."

"Even your *Secret Duchess?*" I could not help asking.

"But she is not *mine*. She is *ours*. Surely you are not jealous?"

"No," I answered slowly. "I was, but I don't think I am any more."

Curiously, it was true. I looked around the cabin, the place where I had been so miserable, so frightened and unhappy, the place which had been my prison, and it no longer seemed like one, but a room of charm, a haven, my home. The mysterious change had come about in large part, I was sure, because the misunderstandings, the barrier between Adam and me had been removed. But I could not help wondering if the Celestial Buddha did not have something to do with it. That fat, smiling god had gone—gone home at last. And Ah Ching, too, would soon be laid to rest. I felt that *The Secret Duchess*, having been purged of these restless, ill-starred spirits, would cease to appear as my rival and become my friend and ally.

As it turned out I was right. Our passage to Sydney and then to Melbourne (where we deposited Bella Kincaid and her pearls), and the long haul back to San Francisco, with the exception of a few squalls, was without event, dull, in fact, but restfully so. Despite all our misfortunes the voyage proved to be a financial success. In addition to our profits from the cargo we received a rather handsome remuneration from Ching's relatives, and from the Buddhist monks, as a token of *their* appreciation, a lovely emerald ring.

But here I am getting ahead of my story.

Adam came and sat down beside me. "I will never forgive myself for placing you and Roxanne in such jeopardy," he said. "It was a horrible mistake."

"We all make mistakes," I said, rather piously, remembering too well my own.

He grinned at me, an impish gleam to his eye. "Hammersmith would say, 'if we are repentant, we shall be forgiven all our sins and mistakes on Judgment Day.' But, as for me, I do not care to wait that long."

"Nor do I," I said, going into his arms.

And we did not.

AVON ⬥ GOTHIC ORIGINALS
MASTERPIECES OF SUSPENSE!

Crucible of Evil   Lyda Belknap Long

Amanda Lescot left her childhood home, Lescot Manor Hall, to escape an evil too horrible to be borne. But in a sudden flash of mysterious and terrifying circumstances, her sinister ordeal began again—leading to a fearsome struggle to overcome dark and mysterious forces!

(19646—95¢)

The Spirit of Brynmaster Oaks
Anne J. Griffin

A beautiful young bride learns of her husband's sinister past—and the terrifying vision that will come to haunt them both—as they are plunged into a strange web of suffocating evil! (19737—95¢)

Stark Island   Lynna Cooper

Inez came to Stark House to catalogue the library, but one night as she took a moonlight swim in Deepdene Pool, she saw a pair of bright eyes watching her from the shrubbery. Thus began her encounter with a horrible creature, and a macabre figure in the family mausoleum! (19463—95¢)

Where better paperbacks are sold, or directly from the publisher. Include 25¢ per copy for mailing; allow three weeks for delivery.

Avon Books, Mail Order Dept., 250 West 55th Street,
New York, N. Y. 10019

**OVER ONE MILLION COPIES SOLD
OF THIS $19.95 BESTSELLER!
NOW AN AVON PAPERBACK—ONLY $7.95!**

This sumptuous 9" x 11⅛" softbound volume contains every word, every picture of the original hardcover edition, reproduced in 304 pages of magnificent color, and sharp, sparkling black and white.

Beautiful photographs you'll instantly remember ... stirring photographs you'll never forget ... all in a stunning big book you'll treasure forever.

> **"A GREAT ANTHOLOGY ... The best pictures
> shown in the magazine's pages through the years.
> LOOK AND RELIVE IT ALL."**
> *Boston Globe*

SELECTED BY THE BOOK-OF-THE-MONTH CLUB

At your nearest bookstore, or use this handy coupon to order by mail.

AVON BOOKS, Dept. BL, 250 West 55th St., N.Y., N.Y. 10019
Please send me THE BEST OF LIFE. I enclose $7.95, plus 50¢ for postage and handling. (Please use check or money order—we are not responsible for orders containing cash. Allow three weeks for delivery.)

Name_____
Address_____
City_____ State/Zip_____